Miss E.

Brian Herberger

Miss E.
by Brian Herberger

Birch Cove Books
Washington, DC

Distributed by Bublish, Inc.

Cover illustration by Michael Gelen, Inkwell Studios
Design by Jeffrey Herberger

Publisher's Cataloging-In-Publication Data
(Prepared by The Donohue Group, Inc.)

Names: Herberger, Brian.
Title: Miss E. / Brian Herberger.
Description: Washington, DC : Birch Cove Books, [2016] | Interest age
    level: 010-018. | Summary: "Being the new kid in town is a way of life
    for Bets, but moving to California in 1967 is different. Her father
    leaves for the war in Vietnam, her history teacher gives an assignment
    that has the whole school searching for clues, and the town's most
    mysterious resident shares a secret with Bets that has been hidden away
    for decades. When a peaceful protest spins out of control, Bets is
    forced to reconsider how she feels about the war her father is fighting
    and her own role in events taking place much closer to home."-- Provided
    by publisher.
Identifiers: ISBN 978-0-9974875-4-1 | ISBN 0-9974875-4-2 |
    ISBN 978-0-9973518-6-6 (ebook)
Subjects: LCSH: Vietnam War, 1961-1975- -Protest movements-- California--
    Juvenile fiction. | Bildungsromans. | High schools-- California--
    History-- 20th century-- Juvenile fiction. | Aeronautics-- History-- 20th
    century-- Juvenile fiction. | Nineteen sixty-seven, A.D.-- Juvenile
    fiction. | CYAC: Vietnam War, 1961-1975- -Protest movements-- California-
    -Fiction. | Coming of age-- Fiction. | High schools-- California--
    History-- 20th century-- Fiction. | Aeronautics-- History-- 20th century--
    Fiction. | Nineteen sixty-seven, A.D.-- Fiction. | LCGFT: Historical
    fiction.
Classification: LCC PZ7.1.H47 Mi 2016 (print) | LCC PZ7.1.H47 (ebook) |
    DDC [Fic]-- dc23

To my mother, wife, and daughter.
I see each of you in these pages.

If you're going to San Francisco
Be sure to wear some flowers in your hair
- Scott McKenzie -

Diary

I promised Miss E. I would never tell anyone her story – and I'm not, really. But she didn't say anything about not writing it down. As far as I'm concerned, a girl's diary is pretty much the most private place someone could ever put something, so writing it here all but guarantees that no one will ever know what really happened to Miss E.

Some diaries stay private because they're locked away in a nightstand or hidden under a mattress, but most of the time they're private because who really has the time to read all the boring stuff that goes on in someone else's life. And as far as boring lives go, mine had to be up there in the top ten, until we moved to California at least. So, there's not much chance of someone prying into my private life.

Although I suppose someone could show an interest after I die.

Seems like people always become more interesting after they're dead and gone, and others end up examining their letters and diaries and just about everything they wrote, trying to find out something about the person that they probably could have found out while they were living by just going up and asking them. But they didn't. Miss E. sure stirred up a lot of attention for herself when she died. Folks probably wouldn't have been half as interested in her if they knew she was alive and well, living on a farm north of San Francisco.

And besides, what I'm writing here isn't really Miss E.'s story. It's mine.

Settling In

When you're an army kid, you know about moving around. I was only fifteen when we moved to California, and that was already the fourth move of my short life. Born in Atlanta, Georgia; moved to Baton Rouge, Louisiana, age two; Amarillo, Texas, age six; Wichita, Kansas, age nine. I really only remember Texas and Kansas.

Texas – flat, dry, hot. I started school there, so maybe that's what I remember the most. Big brick building, lots of noise, kids running around, playing tag, pulling pigtails. I don't really remember any teacher names, which is strange because for a while they seem to become the most important people in your life. Had a friend, Jeanne Hawkins – still remember her name – that I wrote letters to for a while, but to a nine year old, writing a letter is way too much like a school assignment. So that friendship faded away along with my teachers' names. Goodbye Texas.

Kansas – just as flat, just as dry, but thankfully not quite as hot. School was on base, so all the kids knew how friendships work for army kids. There's no time to waste figuring each other out. If we took the five or six months most kids waste sizing each other up and deciding who they want to be friends with, we'd be gone before we said hello. Nope, there's no new kid in a base school. Most are either just getting there or getting ready to leave, so no one stands out as new. You know most kids' names by lunch, and figure out who your best friend will be by the end of the first day so you've got someone to walk home with.

California was different.

California – not flat, not dry, not hot.

California was blessedly cool for a kid who has spent her life thinking it was normal to have a sweat soaked T-shirt on a Saturday morning before the sun got high enough to peek above the roofs and trees. But the temperature was just about the only thing I felt good about when we finished that drive over the mountains and climbed out of our car.

We arrived in early July. My mother told me the move was planned that way so I would have time to settle in before I had to start school, but I knew it was really so my father could help with the unpacking before he had to report for duty. So far I'd been pretty lucky as far as army kids go. Dad had worked on base as a mechanic, making sure planes were well maintained, rebuilding an engine when it got cranky, and even helping the guys in the motor pool when they had a problem with a truck or a jeep that they couldn't figure out themselves. He had a reputation for being able to fix anything, so when it was time for a new assignment, he could pretty much pick the place because everyone had heard of him and they all wanted him turning their nuts and bolts. At least that was how he explained it to me at the dinner table when he was giving me one of his speeches on hard work or reputation.

But like I said, California was different.

In 1967, every kid with a father in the military knew that Vietnam held the trump card. The days of picking where we wanted to move next were over. Uncle Sam was calling up all the boys eighteen and older to wear a helmet and carry a gun, and he wanted my Dad to keep their planes and trucks running. Our move to California wasn't about settling in at a new base where my father would work each day and be home for dinner by five. My father would spend about a month at Oakland Army Base before heading off to Vietnam. Other than delaying a tearful goodbye another thirty days, my mother and I packing our lives off to California was mostly about living close to my aunt and uncle and cousins while we were without my father. I'd never even met them before and only knew about them from hearing my mother complain about them at the dinner table, but we were losing my father for who knows how long, and family is family I suppose.

So I found myself carrying my things into a small rented house outside of Santa Rosa, California, and bringing them into my new room. Pretty much everything I could call my own fit into three boxes. Two were full of clothes and the third held my books, a few favorite toys, and some framed pictures. I hadn't accumulated much over the last fifteen years. I dropped the boxes and turned in a circle to take in my new room. Four white walls, one window, one door, one closet, one bed, one desk. Even though we weren't living on base, the room was totally army issue. My walk from the front door to my room hadn't given me much hope for the rest of the house either.

My clothes hung in the closet and my books moved from the box to the desk, I left my room and found my parents facing each other in the kitchen. My mother looked tearful and my father had his shoulders shrugged and his hands spread apart in front of him. His mouth hung silently open, but his body said, "What can I do." I'd watched my father fix our car countless times, knew it was his job to keep things running smoothly on base, and had lived in the army houses that he'd turned into comfortable homes through his creativity and hard work. Seeing him in the kitchen that day, I realized that he couldn't fix everything.

When my parents noticed I'd entered the room, the scene quickly changed. My mother turned away from me and began moving things from the kitchen counter to the cupboards. My father's what-can-I-do posture turned into a casual lean against the refrigerator, and his expression snapped into a smile.

"What d'ya think, Bets?" My mother always calls me by my given name, Elizabeth. That's an old lady's name. Friends opt for Bethy, which I'm fine with, but Dad's name for me is the only one that ever feels right. Bets.

"It's nice," I lied and then nodded my head and shrugged my shoulders at the same time. Dad and I have always talked with our bodies more than our mouths. My shrug tells him how I really feel, but he knows my nod means I'll make the best of this. Dad returns the expression. Nod. I know how you feel. Shrug. I wish I could fix this. My mother only heard my "It's nice." She'd composed herself and turned with a smile.

"Your father and I were talking about finding a restaurant in town tonight. Take a look around, maybe meet some of the neighbors. How does that sound?"

"Sounds... nice."

Rumours

My first few weeks in California were uneventful and slow. My father went to the base for training each day. My mother took stock of what we had in the house, shopped for groceries and kitchen gadgets, and got invited to the neighbor's for coffee. At first I tagged along hoping there would be kids my age, but after becoming a *de facto* babysitter at a house with two-year-old twins, I cast my social net toward the sidewalks of Front Street and the only pizza place in town.

Forestville, California, is about sixty miles north of San Francisco. Far enough away that I'm quite certain most people in San Francisco had never heard of it, and my guess is there were a few Forestville residents who had never heard of San Francisco. The closest big town is Santa Rosa, but Forestville had a grocery store with a small hardware section, so most people didn't have much need to go very far. The center of town has one of those streets that just has a highway number when you're out in the middle of nowhere and then gets a real name for a couple blocks in town. Between Covey Road and 2nd Street, Highway 116 becomes Front Street, and that's about it. One grocery, one bank, one gas station, and three restaurants. Thankfully, one of them specialized in pizza so that's where anyone under twenty hung out.

Front Street was a short walk from our house and my parents trusted me to head off on my own. It was the height of summer. Far enough into vacation that kids had gotten into their summer routine of sleeping late and then wandering over to the standard meeting places to try to figure out what they wanted to do with the day, yet still enough days of vacation left that no one had yet realized that they'd plodded through an entire summer without ever really doing anything at all.

For the first time in my life, I was settling into a new home with nearly two months of summer to make friends and learn what's what around town before school started. I pushed the real reason for the timing of our arrival in California aside and decided to take full advantage of the weeks ahead. If I played my cards right, I'd have a best friend or two to walk with to school and sit next to at lunch. Worst case, everyone would at least know who I was, and I'd avoid the classroom full of faces turned around in their desk to get a look at the new girl. Another mark in my favor was that I would be starting high school this year. Forestville was only big enough to need one elementary school that went through eighth grade and one high school, so it was likely that most of the kids knew each other since kindergarten. At least we'd all be walking into an unfamiliar school on that first day, but that was still eight weeks away.

My usual approach in a new town was to act cool and comfortable. I figured if I looked like I belonged, then I wouldn't stand out so much as the new kid. This worked for me about half the time. The other half, kids either saw through the act or thought I was being aloof – but I usually stuck with the approach since I didn't think I could better my odds by simply acting like myself. Maybe it was the freedom of a whole summer to make friends, but this time I decided to try something different.

I'd already been to Sonny's with my parents our first night in town, so I knew it was the best place to get pizza. Well, the only place. But when I saw a group of three girls walking down the opposite sidewalk toward Sonny's, I took my chances and crossed the street.

"Hi, my name's Bethy. I'm new in town. Where's the best place to get pizza?" Three short sentences, but they were like cards tossed down on the table. I was totally showing my hand as the new kid in town who didn't have any friends and didn't know her way around, and I was standing there hoping these girls would pick up the cards.

"Sonny's is the only place," said a dark haired girl, gesturing ahead of her down Front Street. They'd only slowed their walk for a second to answer, so I gave a cheerful, "Thanks," and then was left standing on the sidewalk watching them walk away. Rather than follow after them like a puppy dog,

I pretended to take a look at the town bulletin board that stood in front of the grocery. There was a flyer for a yard sale that happened last month, and someone was trying to sell a 1963 Chevy Nova that "Runs Great!" Eventually I continued down the sidewalk toward Sonny's. I wasn't really hungry, but Sonny's sold pizza by the slice, and I can always find room for one slice. Besides, I thought it would seem weird to ask about a pizza place and then not go.

The tables and chairs at Sonny's seemed like an afterthought. Most people either ordered a whole pizza to go, or grabbed a slice and ate it while walking. A lot of the space was taken up by the counter and the small kitchen behind it, but there were a few tables stuck against the wall for those that wanted to stay. I ordered a slice, and while the man behind the counter (I'm not sure if his name was actually Sonny) put it on a plate, one of the girls came up behind me and tapped me on the shoulder.

"Hey, we're here too. Sit with us if you want." She walked off toward one of the tables, and I followed once I had my pizza. I sat down and we all made quick introductions.

Two of the girls were sisters. Cassie was going to be a sophomore, and Anne was going into 8th grade. Susan, the dark-haired girl who pointed me toward Sonny's, was fifteen and would be a freshman. She'd lived in Forestville all her life, but the two sisters had only moved there a few years ago. Susan lived right next to them and had helped them settle in, so all three were sympathetic to me being new in town. They apologized for not stopping to talk while out on the sidewalk and explained how they were trying to avoid a boy who was interested in Cassie. We spent about an hour eating our pizza and slowly sipping Cokes, but mostly talking and laughing while all three filled me in on what school was like, which boys were cute, and what to do around town.

So chalk one up for my new approach to making friends. My first attempt, seemingly a disappointment initially, had actually turned out OK. I'd met three friendly girls who had enough in common with me to carry on a fun conversation, and I'd probably be seeing Susan in classes once school started up. Rather than ignoring me or talking about me behind my back, they decided to embrace me as the new girl and welcome me to town.

Since we all lived in the same direction, we ended up walking down Front Street together. We were just getting up to the section of sidewalk where the bulletin board stood, when Susan stopped and said in a hushed voice, "Miss E." The other girls stopped with her and Cassie put her hand on my shoulder to keep me from going farther. I turned to ask them what was going on, and realized they were all looking down the sidewalk where an older woman was moving toward the grocery store. If we'd kept walking, we would have passed by her on the sidewalk. Instead, we were standing about ten steps from the entrance to the store watching her climb the steps and disappear through the door.

"How long since she's been to town?" Cassie asked, still looking in the direction of the store as if trying to see in through the windows.

Susan shook her head, "I haven't seen her in almost a year."

"Me neither," added Anne, "but I heard some people saw her four or five months ago."

With that, all three girls fell silent. I waited for some explanation. When none came, I finally tried to ask who the woman was, but my question only broke the silence and prompted more discussion from them.

"Want to go in the store?"

"Little rude, don't you think?"

"Why?"

"She's a little odd, but no one deserves to have people following them around gawking. Besides, you really want to spend the day watching an old lady shop?"

The girls stood there for another minute or so in silence and then started walking again. They kept quiet for another block as if they were afraid to talk about the woman while on the same street as her, and then they filled me in.

They gave me the list of things people know about Miss E. It was a short list.

- No one really knows her name.
- People just call her Miss E. Maybe someone knew her name years ago and shortened it to the initial, but no one remembers.
- She lives on a farm about five miles outside of town and only comes into town a couple times each year. When she does come to town, she buys a cart full

of items at the grocery store and doesn't say much other than please and thank you and comments about the weather.

- She surprised the whole town ten years ago by showing up at a church bingo night where she didn't talk to any of the people at her table but left with the $50 prize in her pocket.

- There are only a couple people alive today who remember a time before she lived on the farm, but they were already old back then, so their memories have been so mixed up with the stories that people have told through the years that there's really no telling what's real and what's not.

End of List.

One of the other two restaurants in town was a burger place with a walk-up window that sold ice cream, milk shakes, and sodas. I cemented my newfound friendship with the three girls by offering to buy them an ice cream, and the fact that we all ordered the same flavor – marshmallow fudge – sealed the deal. We sat on a park bench in a grassy area across the street from the building that served as Forestville's town hall, enjoying the ice cream in large licks before it melted down the cones to our hands.

But when the red pickup truck drove slowly by, Susan stopped licking and nudged me with her elbow. I looked up from my cone and knew right away who was driving it. There was a rough tarp covering some boxes in back – presumably her supplies from the grocery, and Miss E. sat up front looking straight ahead and driving at the same slow deliberate pace she'd used walking up the steps to the store. If my father had been sitting on the bench next to me, he would have identified the truck as a Chevrolet from two blocks away and would have shared out loud his guess as to the year. "Looks like a '37 or '38. Maybe a '39, Bets."

There were lots of older cars driving along the streets of Forestville, but watching the red pickup roll by was like stepping back in time. It was old, but it wasn't. It was from another era, but it looked like it had just been bought yesterday, and as it moved down Front Street toward us I was afraid to take my eyes off of it, certain that if I did, I would discover that the town around me had been transformed into a blurry black and white dream image of its past. My gaze followed the truck as it got closer, and then I realized the woman inside was looking back at me. Her head turned, and our eyes met as the truck pulled up to the stop sign in front of us. She probably only stopped for an instant, but having her look at me so intently made it feel like an hour. I was embarrassed to be caught staring, but at the same time, couldn't make myself look away. And in that instant I realized that the woman matched her truck. Old, but not old. So much a part of another time that you felt like she would bring you back with her if you got too close.

From a distance she could have been any other old lady in town. Grey hair, stooped over a bit, walking with an attention that hinted at tired joints and an unsteady step.

But up close I could see details that made her anything but a typical old lady. Her hair had a spring to it, a mop of curls with life in them that hadn't faded with the color. And the wrinkles and creases in her face looked intentional, as if she were putting on a scowl as part of her appearance in town. But her eyes. Her eyes told the whole story. There was youth in them that couldn't be dampened by the grey hair and wrinkles, and the scowl on the rest of her face couldn't cover up what I saw in her eyes.

I wanted to stand up and walk over to the truck to ask her why she was staring at me. I wanted to call to one of the girls sitting beside me to see if they'd even noticed what was going on. I wanted to walk backwards, unable to look away but at least putting some distance between me and the old woman.

And then, the red truck pulled away.

I watched it drive to the top of the low hill where Front Street turned back into Highway 116 and then disappear over it. I watched until I saw the last glint of sunlight on chrome, helpless to do otherwise. The marshmallow fudge had long since reached my hand and was heading for my elbow.

Departure

There wasn't a day since we arrived in California that I hadn't thought about my father leaving. My friendship with Cassie, Anne, and Susan grew in the weeks after I met them. I settled into the daily routine in Forestville, and I made the most of each day knowing that school was fast approaching. But in the back of my mind, no matter what I was doing, there remained an aching reminder that my father would be leaving soon.

Pizza at Sonny's. My father is leaving soon. Board games at Anne's house. My father is leaving soon. Swimming in the creek. My father is leaving soon. Until the day that "My father is leaving soon," turned into "My father leaves today."

My mother hadn't brought up the subject of my father's departure since we moved to California. So as not to break my mother's illusion, my father had his usual smile on as he packed his duffel and got his things ready to load into the car as if he were heading off to another day at the base. But when he looked at me, I could see right through it.

His mouth smiled, but his eyes were saying, "I'm sorry" and "I'll miss you" while his shoulders still hung in the "I wish I could fix this" pose he'd worn for the last month. My mother seemed to notice none of this.

Sometimes it amazed me how my mother could have spent nearly twenty years with my father and still not know how to read him. To me, his expressions and gestures said more than words ever could, and they never lied. No matter what my father was saying, I always knew what he was thinking and feeling just by looking at him. But my mother didn't. I just figured she spent too much time puttering around in the kitchen to actually look at my father when he was talking.

"You want to help me with this, Bets?" my father called as he lifted up his bags, and the quick sideways movement of his head told me that he could carry double the bags without a lick of help from me, but what he really needed was for me to walk outside with him. My mother hummed over the dishes.

I followed my father outside, and after he tossed his bags into the trunk, he closed it and hopped on top, putting his feet on the bumper. From nowhere, or maybe from a back pocket, he produced two Cokes and popped the caps off using the edge of a fender. With a quick tap on the trunk, he called for me to sit beside him and then passed me a Coke when I did.

"I need you to help your mother while I'm gone, Bets."

"But..." I tried to protest, ready to name all the things she should be doing for me, but a silent hand put a stop to my words.

"I know you and your mother don't always see eye to eye," he said taking a sip and then putting his arm around me to pull me closer, "but now's the time to fix that. With me away, your mother's going to need you just as much as you need her."

I opened my mouth to argue again, but a look from my father made me swallow my words and drink the Coke instead.

"Do what needs to be done, Bets, whether it's laundry or dishes or just helping to keep your mother's chin up."

I knew it was the last word on the subject. I'd grumbled to my father before about my mother. To me, it seemed like she was along for the ride. She cooked and cleaned of course, but my father really ran our family. His job and his drive for the next big thing determined where we went and where we lived. And through every new home, every move, she just seemed to do her thing each day and stick to her routine. It was a new town, sure. But they all had a grocery store, all had a lady's club, and neighbors who played bridge and drank coffee. It was me who had to adapt, fill in the gaps, and make up for what my mother didn't do. And what she didn't want to think about. That was the worst of all. Because my mother had no reaction to my father's deployment, no emotion, I felt it all the more. I was filling in the gap again. My father knew how I felt, would have known it even if I didn't bring it up a couple times while we were alone. But our conversations all ended in a pep talk just like the one we were having on the trunk of the car packed with my father's bags. "Help keep your mother's chin up, Bets," had become my father's favorite line. And the worst part was, he knew I'd do it – do anything – for him.

We sat there for a short moment in silence, my father just staring off into the distance with the sun turning his face into light and dark, shadow and bright. On anyone else, the harsh light would have been too much, but on my father, it only emphasized his best features. It made him look like someone on the black and white cover of a magazine. I gave him a quick nod to show I'd go along with his request, and he hopped off the trunk.

"C'mon, Bets. Got something to show you." My father walked around the corner of the house, and I jumped off the car to follow. When I rounded the corner, I saw him standing next to a shining red bike. My feet stopped so quickly they made a scuffling sound in the gravel of the driveway, and my father laughed at my open-mouthed surprise.

I'd wanted a bike for years, but never even had a used one. In Texas, my mother said I was too small, and in Kansas we lived on the base and she said that I didn't need one because everything was so close. Part of me had hoped that the move to California coupled with starting high school might mean a used yard sale find in my future. I'd never dreamed of a new bike.

I took a step closer and ran my fingers along the smooth shining chrome handlebars and then the top of the red frame. I looked my father in the eyes and the smile on his face made mine grow even bigger.

"How did you..? Does Mom..?"

My father laughed again. "She wasn't sure at first, but I convinced her you'd need one if you're going to find a job while I'm away."

My world spun. For the last two years, I'd wanted a job more than I'd wanted a bike even. The chance to take on responsibility of my own, to have a part of my life that wasn't school or home, and of course money in my pocket that didn't depend on a please and thank you to my mother.

"A job? You don't mean it." My father smiled and nodded, then sized up the basket that hung from the handle bars.

"Seems like that basket would be able to carry a fair amount. Might want to stop by Johnson's Grocery tomorrow morning. I may have overheard Mr. Johnson saying yesterday that his last delivery boy left in a rush after he got caught swiping sodas, and that he might be interested in hiring a responsible young lady like yourself."

My only possible reaction was to push the bike aside so I could get to my father and throw both arms around his neck. I squealed a thank you, and he hugged me until my feet were lifted off the ground. But the feel of my father's arms around me somehow reminded me that the bike and the job were a going away present, given to cheer me up (and help me to keep my mother's chin up) while my father was away. I hugged him harder and whispered "I love you, Daddy" in his ear.

He put me down and looked me in the eye. I opened my mouth to tell him one more time that I didn't want him to go, but his voice stopped me.

"I love you too, Bets." And then after a long pause, "I'm not going to pretend that this is a walk in the park." Like your mother, my mind filled in.

"Vietnam's serious business. Boys are dying there. I'm one of the lucky ones because most of the time I won't be where the fighting is. But war's a dangerous place, no matter what your job is. I won't pretend otherwise. So I'll make a deal with you." The expression on my face must have been enough to let my father know that in spite of my dislike for my mother's habit of avoiding the topic, his talk of war and dying was scaring the pants off of me. He smiled a little and crouched down to my height.

"Bets, I'll do everything I can do while I'm away to make sure I come home safe. That's my part. Your part, is that you make each day the best that it can be." He saw the question on my face. "No moping around all day. No feeling sorry for yourself or thinking people should treat you differently because your father's away. Enjoy your bike and all the places it can take you. Work hard at your job, and you'll be surprised at the satisfaction it brings you. And when I come home, you tell me all about it."

My father stood up and put out his hand. "Deal?" A handshake felt too formal, like my father was treating me like a grownup, when all I really wanted right then was to be his little girl.

"Cross my heart," I said tracing an X over my heart then putting my hands on my hips and waiting for him to return the promise. He quickly stood at attention, mimicking my gesture in a stiff and formal way and making the X just below the US ARMY patch on his shirt. Then he laughed and messed up my hair.

"Cross my heart. Now, you go try out that bike, Bets, while I check on your mother. It looks fast enough to fly."

I hopped on but didn't even get my foot on a pedal before my father's voice stopped me. "You're wrong about her you know." I stood straddling my bike, suddenly too uncomfortable to turn around to look my father in the eye. "Your mother knows what's going on, as well as you do," he said reading my thoughts from moments ago. "Only difference is on the outside, Bets."

I turned toward him not sure what words were in my mouth, but it didn't matter. My father was already through the screen door and in the kitchen with my mother.

Transition

Our goodbyes at the airport were uneventful. I kept my chin up, my mother did the same without my help, and my father gave us hugs and kisses and smiles. Tearful goodbyes don't work so well when you're surrounded by a bunch of other kids, and their fathers. My father and I already had our talk on the trunk of the car. There was nothing left to say at the airport. And I couldn't say all the things I wanted to – needed to – say because, of course, my chin was up. The ride home with my mother would not be deemed worthy of a school notebook scribbling, let alone a diary entry.

The next few weeks were a blur. New bike, new job, two weeks and counting until school. With my father gone, I knew I'd need to keep myself busy so I didn't waste any time heading to Johnson's. I stopped by the morning after my father left, riding my bike to town and getting there fifteen minutes before Mr. Johnson even opened his store because I wasn't used to how quickly pedaling could get me around.

Riding my bike was an unimaginable thrill. It wasn't like I'd never ridden a bike before. I had a couple friends in Kansas who would lend me their bikes, but that was just to try out. A quick spin around a driveway or down to the corner and back. But this was for real. Now I was setting off for a destination. I was leaving home, riding along the open road with the wind in my hair, and ticking off miles, each one adding to my sense of freedom. Excitement to surely rival being the first to climb a mountain or fly across an ocean!

Mr. Johnson was expecting me, and instead of lobbying for the job I was crossing my fingers I'd get, I had it as soon as I walked in the door. So I found myself instead following him around the store as he stocked shelves and explained what would be expected of me. When I hopped back on my bike ten minutes later, I was heading out to make my first delivery.

The job wasn't full time, barely even part time, but I couldn't have asked for a better one. I arrived each morning when the store opened, bagged weekly orders that people had scheduled with Mr. Johnson, and then spent the next few hours biking around town back and forth between store and delivery destination. I was done by noon most of the time, and had the rest of the afternoon to slip back into the remaining days of summer vacation with a pocket full of change from tips.

I usually spent the afternoons with Anne, Cassie, and Susan. The first few days after my father left, I went home, thinking that my mother would want the company. But she was either busy in the kitchen or visiting with neighbors. She didn't really seem any different than before my father left, so after the third day, I just figured I'd go my own way and only step in if I noticed signs of her needing a chin-up intervention.

Biking gave me a good chance to get to know more of Forestville beyond Front Street. Actually, there wasn't really much beyond Front Street. Technically, Forestville didn't extend very far beyond the center of town. A couple miles north or west of town was the State Natural Redwoods reserve. Mr. Johnson had a couple of customers who lived out that way, but only one who wanted things delivered. I suppose most people welcome the trip to town. Head south or east of town and there's a whole lot of empty space before you hit Santa Rosa, and anyone living out there probably takes their business to the larger town and leaves Forestville to the locals.

Most kids my age don't worry much about exercise. We get enough just doing what kids do. But if I had needed a way to get in shape, spending my mornings crisscrossing town loaded down with groceries would have been the way to do it. Susan commented after the first week that I looked different, and Cassie joked that El Molino High School didn't have a grocery delivering team, but that I'd be a shoo-in for the track team if I kept it up.

Before I knew it, I'd worked my way through two pay days, treated for pizza three times, managed to avoid my mother most of the time, and eventually found myself enjoying the last few hours of summer once again sitting next to Susan on a park bench enjoying an ice cream cone. Her treat.

Routine

El Molino High School was a dream. The school on base in Kansas was a prison in comparison. El Molino consisted of about ten buildings. Library, gym, auditorium, and various buildings housing classrooms. This layout, spread over forty acres, meant that for many transitions between classes, students were walking outside from one building to another through a sunny but cool California September. No matter what class I'd just endured, English, History, Math, everything immediately faded to sunshine and fresh air once I stepped outside. Communist countries seeking to turn their youth into unquestionable followers should consider similar layouts.

El Molino served several surrounding towns, so any claustrophobia from small town Forestville disappeared once I was at school. There were only so many kids to talk to in Forestville. I'd become friends with three of them, I knew a few more as friends of friends, and recognized all the others even if I didn't know their names. But the high school expanded on the local population times ten. Every classroom held the promise of new girls to become friends with. And boys. Boys!

Here's the thing about base schools. Boys at base schools have fathers who are in the military. Fathers in the military tend to raise boys who are a lot like them. Fathers in the military also tend to be a lot like other fathers in the military. All this adds up to a lot of boys who are just way too much like my father to seem at all interesting in other ways. Not so at El Molino.

My schedule. Period one, Math. This would be a cruel punishment, except the teacher is fresh out of college and seemingly feels the same way as I do when it comes to math before 10:00 AM. She takes it easy on us, and the first half of class seems more like social hour than anything resembling algebra. Period two, Science. Freshman year is Earth Science. Considering we're surrounded by mountains and plains, get winds from the ocean, and straddle a fault that cuts the state in half, we're living right in the middle of units two, three, and four. Period three, History. The teacher wore a tie every day, but the anti-war poster behind his desk hinted at political views that most people in Forestville hadn't embraced yet. Fourth period, Home Ec. I cook, I sew, therefore I am. Lunch, outside, cool and sunny. Fifth period, gym. I don't think any high school student enjoys changing into sweats and a t-shirt in the middle of a school day, but the bike delivery job paid off and I seemed to be at the head of the class when it came to running, jumping, and otherwise exerting myself. Sixth period, English. The teacher comes to class late and goes off on tangents from his tangents. Each day we try to guess who will ask the question that sets the chain reaction in motion. Seventh period, Photography. This one, I lucked into. It's a popular class. The teacher is easy, it's a good way to end the day, and who doesn't like taking pictures. The class is filled with mostly sophomores and juniors, but there are a few freshmen who ended up there because it was the only class that fit their schedule. Lucky me.

After the first two weeks, things settled into a routine. The class work was easy. I've always done well in most classes without much effort, and this year was no different. Susan was in my English and science classes. Although I didn't really make any new close friends, I had a few people in every class who I talked to and never had a problem finding someone to sit with for lunch. This was three steps up from Kansas.

After school I stopped by Johnson's each day. Mr. Johnson was fine with my switching to afternoons once school started. Most of his business came in through the door and he didn't seem like he wanted to go out of his way to encourage deliveries. He was happy to pay me in order to keep those customers who wanted their groceries to arrive at their doorstep, but if he lost a few because their milk didn't get there before noon, he wasn't going to lose sleep over it. Most days, I finished my deliveries with time to spare for a stop at Sonny's, and then I headed for home to take care of homework and dinner with my mother.

Dinner and evenings with my mother those first few weeks of school actually seemed normal. The bits of conversation that had been spread out over an entire day while I was home all the time, were now compressed into an hour or two between school, homework, and bed. She asked about school, she asked about friends, and since everything was new and pretty exciting, I had a lot to talk about.

Once we got into the swing of things though, we slipped back into our usual superficial conversations. She would still ask about my day, but I could tell her attention was elsewhere as I answered. I did the same to her, asking about her day then letting my thoughts wander while she gave me answers that were long on routine and short on detail. After a few days of that, we seemed to realize it would be easier on both of us if we just kept quiet.

I had settled into a routine: school, then work, then home. But to call it a routine doesn't make it sound like much fun. But it was fun! I went to a school that didn't seem like a prison. I had a couple of good friends, a pretty cool job, and money in my pocket. As September slipped into October, one day was pretty much like the next, and I liked it that way. So even though it sounds dull – same old, same old, nothing new, stuck in a rut – you realize how nice a routine really is when something comes along and tips it upside down, especially when two somethings come along in the same day.

There was a buzz in the hallway even before I got to history class. Kids leaving the room were all talking to each other, but clammed up when anyone else got close or tried to start a conversation, which was the opposite of the way things usually worked. Most of the time kids leaving a classroom scattered like crows from a gunshot, eager to find a friend who was in another room, racing to find someone that had the answers to the test in science, or pretending to ignore the boy they had been sitting next to in class for the last forty-five minutes. So before I even entered room 110, I knew something was different.

The room was ringed with black and white photos. The anti-war poster still hung in the front of the room, but everything else had been taken down. The photos were at eye level – or what passed for eye level for a group of teenagers who ranged in height from about four to six feet. Each photo showed a single person, with little else in the background. OK, so Mr. Flynn had redecorated, but that didn't explain all the chatter in the hallway.

He held up two fingers in the V-shaped peace sign that had been finding its way into everyone's hands over the last few years. Most people held it high as if an end to the war were somewhere up above them if they could only reach it. But lately, I'd seen it flashed with an aggressive jab, like a shout for peace, punctuated with an "or else!" A couple weeks into school, Mr. Flynn had adopted it as his signal for quiet.

Those still drifting in took their seats quickly, and we all gave him our attention. Mr. Flynn was the best sort of teacher. He was able somehow to trick his students into being interested in whatever topic he was covering that day. He'd also managed to gain enough of our respect that we actually listened when he asked for quiet or gave us directions, not because he'd threatened us with a trip to the office, but because most of us genuinely liked him and wanted to please him. I imagine the school administration had felt otherwise. He was in his first year at El Molino, and the haircut and shave he'd certainly gotten for his interview had long since grown out.

"One hundred pictures. One hundred Americans. The faces of American History. Our history." Mr. Flynn had a way of speaking when he wanted to add dramatic effect. His sentences shortened, some not even sentences, and with pauses between each, they started to sound like lines in free verse poetry. "Your assignment is simple," he continued, "identify these faces."

There was a murmur in the room as we all looked around. Some were easy: Abraham Lincoln, Teddy Roosevelt, Albert Einstein. Others I was unsure of – was that Franklin Roosevelt or Woodrow Wilson? But most, I had no idea. As I turned my head from side to side looking at each face, I discovered something. The faces alternated male, female, male, female. All the way around the room. Fifty men, fifty women. Clearly Mr. Flynn's list of one hundred important Americans was not pulled from the pages of our history textbook. And though many of the faces staring back at me were white, some were black, Asian, Hispanic, two were clearly American Indian. Pretty significant considering everyone sitting in the classroom looked just like me.

"Your task is simple," Mr. Flynn started again and then proceeded to explain an assignment that did not sound simple at all. "As a class, you need to identify these one hundred Americans. You'll also need to explain in a sentence of twenty words or less why each deserves a place on these walls." Twenty words or less was the sort of requirement that sounded easy but really wasn't. Your average kid would think, "Cool, I only have to write one hundred short sentences." But how do you explain why Abraham Lincoln was important in twenty words or less? Then there were all the faces that I didn't recognize. Finding out who someone is based on their picture was like knowing someone's phone number and trying to find out their name by looking in the phone book. Were we just supposed to start flipping through encyclopedia volumes until we came across someone who looked familiar?

Based on the grumblings in the room, everyone else felt that same way. Mr. Flynn held up his hand again, and we quieted. "British intelligence during World War II deciphered a German code that was so complex it was considered unbreakable. They did it by putting their best people together in a room until a solution was found. You'll do the same. You'll work together as a group, same as my other classes. First class to complete all one hundred Americans wins."

He had said the magic word. Juniors and Seniors are usually motivated to work hard in school because they're close enough to see the next step. Maybe go to college or get an actual adult job. But freshman need a little bit more, and

Mr. Flynn was smart enough to dangle a prize in front of us. "I have a friend who works as a clerk in the San Francisco City Hall. He has offered to give us a tour of City Hall and while we're in San Francisco, we'll take a tour of the city. But he can only accommodate one class. The first class to successfully complete this assignment will go on the trip." Mr. Flynn went on to rattle off a number of places that would be visited on the trip, but he'd already said enough. It didn't matter that we'd be visiting some boring city hall and then playing tourist.

In 1967, San Francisco was the place to go for music. Janis Joplin, Grace Slick, Jerry Garcia, there was no telling who else. And they weren't just playing in clubs, they were living there, walking the streets and hanging out on corners. With a whole day spent crisscrossing the city, we were certain to run into someone.

No amount of peace signs would have allowed Mr. Flynn to control the chaos that ensued. Everyone was immediately out of their seat to get a closer look at the photographs. Paper was pulled from binders and names were jotted down. A group in the corner argued about Franklin Roosevelt. Or was it Wilson? In a gesture that cemented my standing in freshman society, I was pulled into a group that was strategizing the best way to divide and conquer, and my suggestion to meet in the library after school was unanimously accepted.

Pushing for the door as we waited for the bell, I ended up eye to eye with one of the photos. A photo of a woman, I thought in her mid-thirties, maybe around my mother's age. She smiled a big friendly smile, but it didn't show in her eyes. Years of reading my father's expressions made that easy to see. Her eyes looked tired as if she'd been squinting into the sun all day. The woman wore a leather jacket, which seemed normal, but something about the picture made me think it was taken long ago, at a time when a woman wearing something like that would have seemed a little odd. Her hair was a mess, not like a hairdo that had been blown in the wind and ruined. It looked intentionally careless, and something in the woman's eyes said that her appearance was as she wanted it, tussled hair and leather jacket, regardless of what anyone else thought. Her hands planted firmly on her hips added to her resolve. The photographer must have been positioned lower than the woman. She was looking down slightly, and because the camera was pointing up, the background revealed nothing but sky.

In spite of the excitement in the room, Mr. Flynn had the last word. "This is the real world ladies and gentlemen. You work together to accomplish a goal. Each one of you is responsible for the group's success or its failure. And the folks out in the hallway want you to fail so that they can win. Welcome to life."

Leave it to Mr. Flynn to figure out what made us all tick. In a high schooler's mind, there was nothing more powerful than the fear of letting the team down. Forget adrenaline, the only thing moving that runner toward home plate or the halfback to a touchdown was the fear of what he'd face in the locker room if he messed up. The bell rang and we left the classroom. I became part of the chatter in the hallways, but all the way to my next class, I couldn't shake the feeling that the woman's tired squinting eyes were still watching me.

Delivery

The rest of the school day was uneventful other than the new social order that was established by the time we made it to lunch. If someone was in your history class, they were your friend. Although we weren't quite ready to sever ties completely, friends in other history classes were on shaky ground. Thankfully, Susan didn't have Mr. Flynn for history, so I didn't have to avoid her. She came looking for me after lunch to find out why I wasn't at our usual meeting spot, and when I filled her in she offered to help if she could. There was also quite a few history textbooks brought outside for lunch, but it didn't take us long to confirm that Mr. Flynn marched to his own drummer when it came to choosing historical figures. Other than Lincoln, Einstein, and Roosevelt, none of the other people were in there. At least if they were, their picture didn't make the cut.

"Mr. Flynn's crazy. Why does he ask us about stuff that's not in the book?"

"Lots of stuff's not in the book."

"Like what?"

"Vietnam's not in the book."

"Vietnam is happening right now. It's not history. What else?"

"Ninety-seven famous Americans aren't in the book."

Similar conversations were taking place all over campus – either frustration at Mr. Flynn for giving us the assignment, or frustration at the textbook for leaving out seemingly important people. In the first month of school, I'd trudged through four chapters of the textbook and couldn't remember any of it. Something told me I was going to come down in favor of Mr. Flynn's version of American history.

Our first visit to the library didn't reveal any new names, but those who were able to stop by after school agreed it was a step in the right direction, and we were happy with what we'd found. The library had a large biography section, intimidatingly large at first. But after looking at just a few books we realized most had a picture of their subject on the front cover. So we knew just by sliding the book out of its slot whether it was one we needed to flip through. We assigned shelves to each person in our class and each agreed to return as soon as they could to scan their section.

We also discovered that the reference section of the library did not circulate books. This was a comforting thought since any of the other classes could sabotage our efforts with a plain old library card – find an important book and check it out so it wasn't there for the other groups to use. As quickly as we thought of the strategy, we realized it could be used on us. We did see a few people from other classes at the checkout desk and eyed their books suspiciously, but how could we accuse them of doing anything wrong? To anyone not in one of Mr. Flynn's classes, they just looked like a couple studious kids with an interest in history. We thought the non-circulating books on American history might end up being our best resource, but decided to attack the biographies first. I knew I had a few deliveries to make for Johnson's, so I said my goodbyes and promised to be back at the library the next day.

When I walked into the store, Mr. Johnson was talking with a regular customer.

"Don't know. She never has before," I heard Mr. Johnson say as I grabbed the clipboard from its hook on the wall and started to fill a box with the first order."

The woman in front of the counter was talking in a low voice, so the conversation was more like listening to someone talk on the phone. I didn't really care anyway since I was still thinking about the contest in history and the possibility of a trip to San Francisco.

"Ordered the same stuff she usually comes in to buy... Could be. But she didn't sound sick on the phone. Just seemed her regular crabby self... Don't really matter one way or the other as long as the bill gets paid." Then Mr. Johnson noticed me down the aisle and called me up to the counter.

"Elizabeth, got a delivery here that needs to go out today. Bit of a trip, so you best take care of it first. It's already boxed and ready to go." He handed me a slip of paper with the address on but it wasn't a street I knew and there was no name. Mr. Johnson must have read the confusion on my face. "You'll want to take route 116 about two miles out of town. You'll see a narrow dirt driveway on the right. That'll take you by the house. Only house on it, so you can't miss it." I reached for the box, but Mr. Johnson was resting his hand on it, so it stayed frozen there for a moment like we were playing tug-a-war with it.

"Your mother OK with you riding that far out of town?" I shrugged off the question and nodded, but the look in Mr. Johnson's eyes told me that he wasn't really worried about my mother. I left the store confused, but once I was on my bike, I let my mind wander and enjoyed the scenery on the outskirts of town. I found the dirt road right where Mr. Johnson said it would be, and I only had to bike on it for a minute or two before I came to the top of a hill and saw a farmhouse and barns nestled in a field just ahead. And there, parked in front of the house, was the red pickup.

My bike skidded in the dirt and stopped amid a dusty cloud. Now I understood the conversation in the store, Mr. Johnson's hesitation, and the slip of paper with no name. I was delivering groceries to Miss E. I stood straddling my bike in the middle of the road, deciding what to do. But there wasn't really much to decide. People in town seemed to step out of her way, and no one really knew much about her, but I certainly wasn't going to turn around and head back to Johnson's because I was afraid to deliver groceries to an old lady. I put my feet back on the pedals, coasted down the hill and came to a stop next to the pickup.

A peek inside gave me that eerie step back in time feeling again. The interior of the truck was in perfect shape, just like the outside. Old and outdated, and at the same time, new like yesterday. The house on the other hand was clearly from a time long gone. It looked like it was painted white once, but the slivered wooden siding had long since shed the paint and faded to a dull silvery gray. The porch sagged with the weight of time and the boards creaked as I walked across it to the door.

The inside door hung wide open, and through the screen door I could see an entry hallway, but looking in from the bright day, the rest was shadowy. With the box of groceries tucked under one arm, I raised my other hand to knock on the screen door when I noticed the envelope stuck between it and the door frame. I pulled it out and read the front.

LEAVE IT

I opened the unsealed envelope enough to see that there were a few bills inside it, but didn't bother counting them. Mr. Johnson never told me what the total was for the groceries I delivered. Some customers gave me money, others didn't and must have had an account. I just delivered and didn't ask.

I peered through the screen door again, then looked back at the envelope, and then at the box of groceries under my arm. I bent down to place the box on the porch, and when I did my face came close enough to the screen that the bright sunlight was blocked out and my eyes started adjusting to the dark. I saw further down the hallway, stairs going up, a doorway into another room – maybe a formal sitting room from the looks of the high chair back and rug on the floor. I could hear faint music, something old and scratchy. Looking through the screen gave a texture to everything I could see, like standing a little too close to a painting and seeing the lines of the brushstrokes instead of the scene the artist intended. And like a painting, everything was still, a captured moment in time. Then I noticed a hand move onto the arm of the chair, the fingers bouncing lightly to the music.

I was so intent on peering into the house my face was pressed against the screen and my hands were leaning on the door, when I saw the movement on the chair I jumped back and the screen door came with me, snapping closed a second later with a bang. My feet were frozen to the porch, the envelope was still clutched in my hand, and my mouth hung open as wide as my eyes. My jump back landed me in the sunlight again, so I could no longer see inside, but I could still hear the music playing. And above that came a voice, calm but forceful enough that I could hear it clearly from outside the house.

"Note said to just leave it."

My mouth opened again to reply, but nothing came out. My feet stepped slowly backward and I somehow navigated the porch steps in reverse. I threw a leg over my bike and was back to the main road before I knew it. My head cleared as I pedaled back toward town and I replayed the incident on the farmhouse porch.

I wondered how many kids in school even knew where Miss E. lived, let alone had actually been there. Granted I hadn't actually been in the house, but based on Cassie's curiosity when we saw Miss E. in town during the summer, I was guessing the front porch was a lot farther than most kids had gotten. I was already planning the story I'd tell the next day in school, when I realized the story also included a rather embarrassing backwards scramble between front porch and bike. I was willing to admit to myself that the sight of an old lady's hand and the five words she spoke to me from inside her house were enough to scare me three steps back, but I wasn't about to let that get spread around town.

By the time I reached the edge of town, I resolved to keep the story to myself. I hopped off my bike and walked back into Johnson's to start boxing the next order, and Mr. Johnson looked at me with raised eyebrows.

"Everything go OK with the delivery?" He asked as I handed him the envelope.

"Sure," I said. "What could go wrong?"

I must have managed to hide my mix of embarrassment and excitement because Mr. Johnson only nodded and turned back to the book he used to keep track of accounts.

Routine Revised

The two events that threatened to upset my routine a few weeks before had now become part of it. Everyone in my history class got to room 110 early so we could scan the pictures again and check them against anything we'd found the previous afternoon. We were now up to sixteen names, and even though things had slowed down after knocking off the easier ones in the first few weeks, we were still getting one or two a week. We weren't sure exactly where the other classes were, but we felt good about our progress.

And on the Miss E. front, a trip out route 116 had become a part of my regular weekly delivery schedule. Each time the envelope was sticking out from the screen door, and each time I just left the box without lingering or trying to look inside the house again. I guess Miss E. had decided I'd learned my lesson on the first delivery. There were no instructions on any of the other envelopes.

Mr. Johnson was obviously curious, and my return was always met with an attempt on his part to strike up a conversation. I never let things lead anywhere though and responded to his statements about the weather or the nice views outside of town with a simple "yep" or an "uh, huh." At that point, I didn't really have any secret to keep, but I felt special since out of everyone in town, I was really the only one who had set foot on Miss E.'s farm since anyone could remember. So acting like I knew something made me feel like someone special, even though I didn't really know any more than anyone else in town, except that Miss E. liked listening to old records and that two of the boards on her front porch squeaked. So what was out of the ordinary a few weeks ago had become my day to day, and I was feeling like things were back to normal. Until the afternoon of the fight.

On the friend front, Cassie had been avoiding a boy on the day I had met her, and he was still paying her more attention than she was interested in getting from him. Peter Anderson had set his sights on Cassie at the end of their freshman year, and he wasn't giving up despite Cassie's consistent refusal to go to the movies with him or to let him walk her home and carry her books.

Even though Forestville was too small to avoid someone entirely, she had an easier time of it over the summer since she could go wherever she wanted and usually went in the opposite direction if she saw him. But once school started back up, it was harder to avoid him. He had learned her schedule and knew where he had to hang out to run into her between classes. Cassie had changed her route to try and avoid him, but there were only so many ways you could get from point A to point B. When she did run into him, he would trail after her trying to strike up a conversation, complimenting her on her outfit, and generally being a pain. He was also ruining her chances with any other boy, since they were walking down the halls together so often, people just started assuming they were dating.

By the time we'd made it to November, Peter was causing some real problems. In her attempts at avoiding him, Cassie was trying more elaborate routes to her classes and was ending up tardy more often than not. She knew the class changes when she was likely to run into Peter and spent so much time worrying about getting to her next class that she couldn't concentrate on the one she was in.

All of this came to a climax outside the auditorium building a couple weeks after I'd started delivering to Miss E. Cassie was part of a drama club production and was on her way to practice. Peter knew her practice schedule and had started lingering outside the building waiting for her each afternoon. I was on my way to the library and, knowing that she was probably going to cross paths with Peter, I offered to walk with her to practice.

As predicted Peter was waiting by the auditorium building doors as we approached. He looked at ease, half-leaning against the side of the steps, his legs stretched out in front of him and his hands stuffed into his pockets. Some of the boys had started letting their hair grow longer, imitating the musicians we admired and the older college students who had started making their way into the news for the trouble they were stirring up over Vietnam. Peter had joined the trend, and his hair hung down in his eyes so he had to push it to the side to see. When he did, he saw us and called to Cassie.

She gave him a short reply about being late for practice, but as usual Peter didn't take no for an answer. He stepped in front of her and peppered her with questions about movies and parties that weekend. She tried to get around him, but each time he anticipated her dodge and moved to block her way.

I don't really know why I got involved. I walked to class with Cassie whenever we were headed in the same direction, and I'd encountered Peter's persistence before. I found it annoying and awkward and felt sorry for Cassie, but I never really took it personally until that day in front of the auditorium. Maybe I was frustrated by our lack of recent progress in history, maybe I was just irritable from the cold I was fighting, or maybe it was the gap in letters from my father. Whatever prompted it, the injustice of what Peter was doing to Cassie finally hit home and felt personal.

"Hey!" I shouted, and when there was no response, I took a step forward so there was no question about who I was talking to and shouted again. The second time Peter took notice and stopped pestering Cassie long enough to turn toward me.

"Leave her alone. She's not interested in you and is tired of you stopping her between classes. Get away from her and stay away."

There was a blank expression on Peter's face as he processed what I'd just said, and he was clearly surprised at my verbal attack. Then I saw his eyes dart side to side, getting in a quick count of the bystanders who had witnessed the exchange, and I understood immediately where Peter was coming from. It wasn't just about being interested in Cassie. Tagging along after a girl for the last two months, Peter had put himself at risk of being labeled as the kid who got dumped before the first date, and I'd just pointed a spotlight at him. But he was used to fending off Cassie's protests, so he quickly recovered and turned things his way. A smile grew across his face.

"Awww, that's so cute, sticking up for your friend. Or maybe you're jealous? I see you a lot with her in the halls. You getting tired of me asking her out instead of you? Well, there's a good movie showing this weekend. If you're interested..."

That's as far as he got. I didn't really think about punching him. I just felt a shift, from feeling sorry for Cassie and being aggravated at the delay on my way to the library to being overwhelmingly angry at the kid in front of me. Angry at how he was messing things up for Cassie, but mostly angry at how he was talking to me. Like I'd be honored to spend time with him. Of course, I thought about all this after, mostly while I was sitting in the principal's office. In that instant what I was really thinking about was just hitting Peter's face with my fist as hard as I could.

And I did.

He was one hundred percent not expecting it. From the tone of his voice, he thought he had the upper hand and was winning our little exchange. Clearly getting punched in the face by a girl was the last thing on his mind. My fist came up from his left, hitting him on the side of his face just under his cheekbone. He actually spun around. Spun around like he was in some cartoon, and when he faced me again his expression had gone from confident smugness to a mixture of surprise and unconsciousness. Peter's mouth hung open and his eyes widened. Then his eyelids flickered and closed, while his body slumped to the ground.

What came next was a blur. I heard a girl's voice cry out, probably Cassie's. A couple boys who were standing around watching let out what could have been a cheer or a yell of surprise. People who were nearby went running to tell others, and those that were farther away came running up to see what had happened. But the crowd gathering around me was peripheral. My attention had been entirely focused on Peter's face, and when he took a nosedive for the pavement allowing me to see beyond the space he'd just occupied, what I saw was the red pickup parked at the curb.

The window was rolled down and Miss E. was leaning on the door looking right at me. Almost like she knew Peter would be knocked out of the way and sat there waiting for the chance to look me in the eye. She lifted her head upward, in a funny sort of nod that seemed only to go up and not down again. Not a nod of approval, more like a nod that just said, "Hey, I see you. Got my eye on you." Then her face disappeared from the window, replaced by an elbow resting on the door, and she threw the truck into gear and drove away. I just stood there and watched it go, my head slowly pivoting until the truck disappeared behind one of the school buildings. Then my attention snapped back to the scene around me.

There were a lot of people. Fights weren't all that common at El Molino I guess, so any scuffle drew attention. Bonus if the fight involved a girl, especially one who just knocked a kid a foot taller than her to the pavement. Most people were just standing around still trying to figure out what had happened. Some were hunched over Peter to see if he was OK, others were comforting Cassie, probably thinking that she was upset because the boy they assumed was her boyfriend had been hurt. No one really came up to me, although most were sneaking glances in my direction. I did see a few girls hiding smiles and nodding approvingly, one bold enough to look me in the eyes and show a quick thumbs up partially hidden against her chest.

Cassie finally shook off the shock and rushed over to hug me.

"Sorry," I mumbled into her hair. Not because I'd hit her boyfriend like half the people gathered around thought, but because unless you're a football jock or a prom queen, no one in high school likes having the spotlight on them, and I didn't just put it on Peter. With one swing, I'd put it on all three of us.

Cassie shrugged. "At least Peter Anderson won't be bothering me in the hallways again," she said with a half-smile.

"At least not while you're around." We shared a quick uncomfortable laugh, then covered our mouths, both realizing that laughing while standing over still knocked out Peter didn't make us look so good.

Someone had gone to get a teacher. There was a shout from the direction of one of the other buildings and everyone scattered. Cassie and I were left standing over Peter, who conveniently came to as the teacher arrived on the scene.

"What's going on here?" the teacher questioned while catching his breath and looking around for Peter's attacker, someone bigger and stronger, someone with enough muscle to knock him to the ground. Peter shook his head as if to clear it and managed to croak out "She hit me." The teacher still looked around at the retreating students before Peter's words sunk in. Finally, he turned to me.

"You... you hit him?" he asked, looking like the facts still didn't add up.

"He's constantly bothering Cassie." I blurted out. "He's a pain. He's always..."

Peter started to interrupt, but I took a step toward him and he scrambled to his feet and scurried away from me.

The teacher pretended to brush an itch on his nose in order to hide a smile. "Well, uhh... you'll need to come with me then." I fell in line behind him as he marched me inside.

I can't say much about the principal's office, because nothing really happened there. I suppose the principal didn't know what to do with a girl who had beat a boy in a fight. He asked a few questions and then had me wait outside his office. I tried to explain about the problems Peter was causing for Cassie, but he didn't want to hear any of that. Mostly, I think what he wanted was to get rid of me and the problem that had landed on his desk just as he was getting ready to go home. But he needed to do something, and that something was to call my mother.

I sat waiting until my mother arrived. Her response was simple. She told me that my father wouldn't approve. That was it. She was neither upset nor not upset. Her only reaction was to let me know what my father's reaction would have been. Our car ride home was silent, not because of silent disapproval, but because my mother was responding to my fight the same way she'd responded to my father's leaving for Vietnam or anything else for that matter – no response at all. I welcomed the silence as a chance to replay the afternoon's events in my mind. Not the fight, but rather the red pickup truck and its driver sitting there watching me.

For a woman who had kept to herself for as long as anyone in town could remember, I was certainly seeing my fair share of Miss E.

Introductions

The fight was on a Thursday, which was the best possible day for it. People were actually calling it "the fight" which was an indication of how rare an occurrence it was. To me, a fight should have a little bit more to it than one punch. Calling it "the afternoon that Bethy Wells hit Peter Anderson so hard he spun around in circles before collapsing to the ground" was more accurate, but a little cumbersome. Regardless, it was on a Thursday, and that was a good thing.

That really only gave us one day to be in the spotlight. And if you had to be in the spotlight, Friday was a pretty good day to be in it. People talked about the fight all morning. Those who saw it, told others what had happened. Those who weren't there talked to others who weren't there as if they were there. So by the end of second period, everyone I walked past between classes had some sort of reaction. The girls were divided into three camps: those who disapproved and thought my behavior way out of line for a girl (these were mostly the cheerleaders and the girls who wished they were cheerleaders), those who approved but didn't want to admit it, and those who approved and wished they were the ones that had taken a swing at Peter. The boys were much simpler. The ones who were friends with Peter were angry at me, and the rest were suddenly curious.

One would think that these were pretty good results for a girl who was relatively new to town and in her first year of high school. Two thirds of the girls admired me and nearly all the boys were elbowing each other out of the way to see who'd get up the nerve to be the one to ask me out first. But like I said before, no high school kid wants that much spotlight, so I was lucky it was Friday.

By noon most of the talk had turned to weekend gatherings and who was going to win the big game against Santa Rosa on Saturday. By seventh period, there were enough weekend plans buzzing around classrooms that most kids had forgotten about "that girl who hit some guy yesterday."

By Monday, everything had blown over. The football team won on Saturday and more than a few kids had done something foolish at a weekend party, so the spotlight had moved on. Peter didn't bother Cassie anymore. In fact, we rarely saw him between classes. It seemed like roles had been reversed and he was actually going out of his way to avoid Cassie and me by choosing alternate routes between classes.

So by Wednesday, I had pretty much forgotten the whole thing until I showed up at Johnson's after school and realized there was an order for Miss E – Miss E. who had been there watching. As I biked toward her farm, I wondered about that. Was she there all along? Or was she just driving through and stopped when she saw there was a problem? If she was sitting there watching and waiting, that was just weird. Who sits around watching school kids go from class to class? By the time I'd reached the dirt road, I decided that it was just a coincidence. She must have stopped for some other reason, and just happened to be there when Peter went down. If she hadn't stopped at that moment, it would have been another car, or no one. And the only reason I had any reaction at all was just because she's an old woman who keeps to herself and has everyone in town wondering about her whenever she does come to town. So it was a coincidence, just like the two of us deciding to stare at each other while she drove through town was a coincidence.

Once I stopped my bike in front of her house and hopped off with her groceries, I had myself convinced of that theory and had decided that this would be a delivery like any other delivery and that her watching me punch Peter didn't matter.

I believed that all the way up to her front porch until I saw that there was no envelope sticking out the door.

I stood in front of the door considering my options. I could leave the groceries like I always did, and just let Mr. Johnson know that there was no payment this time. His problem right? Except I'd have to explain why I didn't knock on the door like I would for any other customer. I could take the groceries back to Mr. Johnson, but again I'd have some explaining to do. The only option that didn't have me making excuses to hide the fact that I was nervous about knocking on an old lady's door, was option three, which required me to actually knock on her door.

I took a deep breath, and did just that. The knock sounded old and rattly, like the door hadn't been knocked on for quite a while. Above the faint sound of the music I'd gotten used to hearing anytime I delivered to Miss E., came the voice I'd only heard once before on my first visit.

"Door's open. Might as well come in off the porch 'stead of standing there. I'm in the kitchen, which is right where you can bring those groceries." It was a voice that got right to the point, in words as well as tone, but not in an unpleasant way, only like it was telling you just what it needed to. And by the time it got done telling, you found yourself wishing it had more to say so you could keep hearing it.

I fumbled for the handle while holding the box and ended up letting the door slap closed once before I was able to wedge my foot in to push it open. I stepped inside and found myself standing in the entryway that I'd tried to peek at through the screen on each of my deliveries. I immediately had that back in time feeling I'd sensed while seeing Miss E.'s truck drive through town, except now I was sure I had time traveled. Nothing around me came from the present. The house and all its contents were from another time.

I walked slowly down the hallway headed toward the back of the house where I guessed the kitchen was and where the voice I'd heard seemed to come from. The walls were lined with old black and white photographs. They looked like newspaper or magazine prints, but these were the real deal. Originals, not clipped from a magazine. A few even had signatures like they had been autographed by whoever was in them. Miss E. must be a collector I figured.

A lot of the photos seemed to show the same woman, sometimes dressed up in a formal setting, but most taken outside with the woman in casual pants and a leather jacket, a scarf tied around her neck. In some photos the woman was standing on the wing of an airplane, and one that caught my eye had her posed in front of a larger airplane with two engines, her arms outstretched with her hands just touching the tip of a propeller on either side. But most of the photographs showed her posing with other people, and these were the ones that had been signed. Signatures I could barely read and names I didn't know. Gore Vidal, Fred Noonan, Harriet Quimby, Louise Thaden, Helen Richey. In one photo the woman was standing together with another woman who was smiling like her teeth were too big for her mouth. Both women wore hats and furs, and the signature on that one was Eleanor Roosevelt. Eleanor Roosevelt? How does an old woman who lives on a farm in middle of nowhere California get her hands on a signed photograph of Eleanor Roosevelt? And who was the other woman that she seems to be such a big fan of?

I tried to put the pieces together, but the voice from the kitchen startled me and nearly made me drop the box of groceries.. "You going to deliver those groceries or did you get lost in the dining room and decide to eat them?"

"Sorry. Um... coming." I started off for the kitchen again, trying to get a look at more of the pictures as I walked by. On the left, I passed the living room where I first saw Miss E. (or more accurately her hand) listening to music and then the dining room on the right. The hallway ended at the kitchen, and when I walked in Miss E. was sitting at a table holding a mug in her hands.

A lot of houses have a certain smell to them, not a bad thing, just the way they smell. Probably the food cooked there, the laundry detergent used, and just the smell that happens as a building ages, all combined together. Something the people who live there never notice because they smell it all the time, the same way, after a little while, a visitor wouldn't notice it anymore. But Miss E.'s house was smell-less. I felt like I was in a museum, like the rooms I was walking by were behind glass, or like I was watching a movie where the camera slowly moved down the hallways turning from room to room, and I was just viewing them without really being a part of them. Until I reached the kitchen.

I guess maybe it was because Miss E. was sitting there, so there was some life to the room. But the kitchen was brighter than the rest of the house and felt alive. When I stepped into it, I felt like I was becoming a part of it, not just standing on the outside looking in. And there was a smell. I couldn't figure it out at first until I saw the red-orange liquid in Miss E.'s mug. Tomato juice. Who drinks tomato juice? I mean, I guess if you're in a hurry and need something on the go, but sitting at the kitchen table?

"Figured at some point, we best make some introductions. Can't have someone coming to my house every week or so without my even knowing her name."

I hesitated, still taking in the room and wondering why the woman who didn't talk to anyone in town had invited me into her kitchen to make introductions. My mother had hammered into me the lesson about not talking to strangers. My father was more likely to step up, shake a stranger's hand, and turn them into an acquaintance. But Miss E. wasn't really a stranger. I mean, everyone in town knew her, or at least knew of her. And she was a customer, and I always talked to them.

"Elizabeth," I said but I looked down at the floor as I did. That's how I introduced myself to adults, but at that moment it didn't feel right. "But friends call me..."

"What do you call yourself?" Miss E. interrupted, and I realized that Bethy wasn't right either. A name for formal and a name for friends, but neither seemed to fit what was happening in her kitchen.

"Bets," I finally said firmly, and took a step forward to put out my hand.

"Well now, there's a name you seem comfortable with," Miss E. said. "Who gave you that one?"

From the laugh in her voice I thought she was teasing me about the nickname but when I defensively told her that my father gave it to me she stood and shook my hand. "Well, he got that one right, didn't he? Bets it is then. Please to meet you, Bets."

She walked away from me then, taking some things from the box and distributing them to the cupboards. I waited uncomfortably for her to introduce herself, and she finally said with her back to me, "Folks in town tell you my name?"

I hesitated. "They call you Miss E." I said and quickly added, "But what do you call yourself?"

The kitchen was filled with her laughter as she enjoyed the irony of being caught in her own question, and it was the kind of laugh that you couldn't help but join in with. It must have been a full minute before the two of us settled down. Finally Miss E. sighed and caught her breath and looked me in the eye.

"Thanks for that one, Bets. Haven't laughed like that in a while. As for my name, you've probably talked enough with the townies to know that no one's really called me by my proper name since any of them can remember." There was a long pause. Long enough that I thought I should say something and took in a breath to say it when she started again.

"Meelie. Mostly I call myself Meelie. My little sister gave me that name, and it stuck." On anyone else it would have sounded like an old lady's name, and it was a perfect fit for a woman who drove an old truck and lived in an old farmhouse. But that name hanging on the woman who was standing across from me in the kitchen sounded instead like a little girl's name. Which seemed odd until I realized that I'd still call myself Bets when I was seventy, or eighty, or ninety. Nicknames had a way of sticking with people no matter how old they got.

I wanted to greet her by name and shake her hand again, but I didn't need my mother to tell me that my father wouldn't be pleased with me calling a seventy-year-old woman by her nickname.

"Uhh... Ma'am," I hesitated, "I don't think my parents would approve of me calling you Meel... uhh, me calling you that."

"Course they wouldn't. They'd be horrible parents if they did. But Ma'am won't do either. I've certainly never been a Ma'am to anyone. What did you say they call me in town?"

"Well... they call you Miss E.," I said quietly.

She thought about it for a moment. "That'll do, Bets. Now, you best be getting back to town or people will start wondering where you are." Miss E. took an envelope from her counter top and handed it to me. "And I don't imagine most folks in town would care one way or the other if they found out you'd made my acquaintance, if you catch my meaning."

I understood and nodded. I hadn't told anyone about the day Miss E. drove by in the red pickup, or about seeing her the day of the fight. It wasn't that I was hiding anything, just that it didn't seem like someone else would understand. Plus it felt like something unique that had happened to me and only me, and I was pretty sure talking about it would let that feeling slip away. The visit to Miss E.'s house felt the same way. I wasn't sure why she wanted it kept a secret, but I'd already decided I wasn't going to tell. "Swell right hook you've got," she said from behind me as we left the kitchen. I felt myself blush a little and was glad to be facing away from her. I could stand firm against the principal or my mother and defend what I'd done to Peter that day, but Miss E. mentioning it made me feel embarrassed and a little guilty. Maybe because she'd been there to see it. Miss E. continued. "Looked like you made quite a stand for women's rights that afternoon, huh Bets?"

I hadn't really thought about the fight that way. Peter was bothering Cassie, and I made him stop. Miss E.'s comment put things in a different light, made it seem bigger than I thought, but I was still sorting it out in my head, so I changed the subject.

"I like your collection."

"Collection?"

"Your collection of old photographs."

Miss E. laughed. "Well, those photographs might seem old to you."

"And the autographs! Eleanor Roosevelt?"

She smiled. "Now, she was an amazing woman, that Eleanor. You can be sure of that, Bets."

I liked that she kept calling me by name even though we were the only two there and I knew she was talking to me. My father did the same. "But where did you get them? Where did you get Eleanor Roosevelt?" Maybe it was just because it was the only name I recognized. But I remembered reading about Eleanor Roosevelt years ago in a library book about all the First Ladies. I read and reread the chapter on her because I thought she was more like a real person than any of the others. So seeing an autographed photo of her made her seem even more real. It fascinated me.

"Well, Bets. I'll see you again next week with the groceries," Miss E. said in answer to my question, and before I knew it I had been ushered outside and was looking back at Miss E. through the screen door. She gave me a smile and turned to walk back down the hallway.

"Why me?" I called after her. She only half turned with a raised eyebrow, so I repeated my question, and when she gave me a confused look I continued. "There's a town full of people who you ignore. You don't talk to any of them, you don't invite any of them into your home. So why suddenly start having your groceries delivered? Why today stop putting the envelope in the door?" I paused. "Why me?"

She laughed again, that same laugh that had filled the kitchen, except this time I felt like I wasn't in on the joke. "Aww, Bets. You haven't figured that out yet?" I could only shrug my shoulders and shake my head. "Because you remind me of myself when I was your age." With that she turned and disappeared down the hallway, leaving me to peer through the screen door into darkness like I had each week before.

Puzzle

Room 110 was chaos. It had been discovered that students were trading answers with people in other classes. It was a complex system that rivaled the stock exchange. Photographs had been given point values based on how difficult they were considered, taking into account the relative fame of the person in question and the available resources that could be used to identify them. Then they were swapped on an open market, some difficult photos trading for three or even four photos of lower point values.

That alone was not what turned history class into a riot scene though. Trading answers between classes felt like nothing more than helping each other with homework. Some kids understood math, others were a wiz at grammar. There were always clusters of students outside before first period comparing answers and sharing the correct ones. But what had turned the classroom upside down in early December, was that many of the answers that had been traded were wrong. It seemed that some of the most valuable photos, the ones that had traded for three or four others turned out to be fakes. So kids had given away some of their best answers and had gotten nothing in return. The worst of it was that there had been so much trading and swapping around that no one could be certain where the fake answers had come from. Those who were accused just passed the buck and said they had gotten it from someone else.

We spent the rest of class sifting through the answers we had, trying to toss out the ones we now knew were wrong, putting any that had been gotten through a trade into a questionable pile, and sizing up the dwindling number of photos that we knew were correct because we had discovered the answers ourselves.

Through it all, Mr. Flynn sat quietly at his desk grading papers. He didn't make any peace signs in an attempt to quiet us down, nor did he do anything to help us sort out the mess. From the slight smile on his face, it almost seemed as if he'd expected the whole trading fraud from the start and let it happen in order to create a learning experience. Mr. Flynn was sneaky in the best sort of way, and had somehow tricked us into learning a life lesson simply by letting us make our own poor decisions.

We were back to less than forty names that we were sure of, and as we got closer to the end of the period, the mood had changed from chaotic to sullen. We had tried various methods of research. Our trips to the library had been initially fruitful, but the Forestville library only held so many books, and it certainly felt like we had sifted through all of them.

Katie Johnson had a small Kodak camera and had spent an hour after school taking a careful picture of each photograph. The film and developing cost a bundle, but split between every kid in class it was manageable. The idea was that we'd have an easier time matching faces if we could hold them side by side, rather than finding a picture we thought was a match only to decide it wasn't when we got back to school and compared. The results were encouraging and we got three new names the week the pictures came back from the developer. But we quickly found the flaw in the idea. We were sharing one hundred pictures among twenty four kids in the class. Someone could easily come across a match and never know it because someone else happened to have the picture. We eventually put all of Katie's prints into two albums: one for men and one for women and that at least gave us a quick reference if we were at the library or flipping through old magazines at home.

Magazines were another brainstorm. Bobby Wilson's parents had stacks of them dating back to the 30's and 40's. They smelled like the basement they had been in for decades, but they were mostly all pictures and we found nine or ten names after spending just a couple days flipping through them. There were piles that we hadn't gone through yet, and we made it a weekly task to go through as many as we could. But it was slow progress. Mixed in with all the pictures were articles and ads, and research sessions usually ended in giggles about unfashionable outfits or predictions of expeditions to Mars.

We tried asking other teachers and parents if they recognized any of the people in the photographs, but Mr. Flynn had clearly briefed all the teachers. They all gave the same canned response. "Nope, never seen him" or "No idea. Do you know who she is?" Parents were so little help, we suspected Mr. Flynn had somehow gotten to them as well.

Waiting for the bell to ring, I used the last thirty seconds of class to scan the faces on the wall. Pretty much every kid did it, hoping one of them would stick in our memory and we'd come across a match. My eyes skipped over the ones I knew we had already and rested longer on the ones we didn't. I came to the smiling woman with squinting eyes. The one with the leather jacket and mop of hair.

I let out a cry of surprise just as the bell rang. Chairs pushed back from desks and no one heard me. So no one knew I had just discovered a match. Well, almost a match, but close enough that I was sure it would be. She was the woman in the pictures hanging on Miss E.'s wall. When I realized it, I wanted to kick myself for not making the connection earlier when I was in her house, because now it seemed so obvious. I stood up to leave, but my gaze was stuck on her. The woman's smile at that moment seemed proud, like she was encouraging me, like she was looking right at me saying, "Go ahead. You've almost got it. Who am I?"

"Elizabeth, are you going to make it to your next class?" Mr. Flynn startled me out of the staring match I was having with the photo.

"Yeah... I mean, Yes, Mr. Flynn." I stammered and started to walk out.

"Good luck with her," he called after me. "No one has figured her out yet."

I turned and smiled as I left knowing how close I was. I could wait for my next delivery and ask Miss E. about the woman in all her photos, but I had a feeling she wouldn't be any more help than the teachers had been. Not because Mr. Flynn had talked to her, but mostly because she seemed like the kind of grown up that would tell a kid to go out and find their own answer rather than making it easy and just telling them. She and Mr. Flynn should go out for coffee. Besides I already knew how I was going to find the missing piece to the puzzle, and the hardest part was going to be just keeping it to myself until after school.

I wasn't really sure why I didn't tell anyone else. Until that point, everyone was so eager for answers, we shared any scrap we came across. Maybe it was our discovery of the fake answers that made me want to be one hundred percent sure before I told anyone, but I think mostly it was the excitement of knowing something that was just for me. Like meeting Miss E.

I made it through the rest of my classes and went straight for the library when school let out. By that time, my feet took me to the biography section like an autopilot. My eyes skimmed the shelves looking for the book I knew was there. We'd already pulled it from the shelf, confirmed that the woman in the cover photo wasn't hanging on Mr. Flynn's wall, and pushed it back in.

I walked down the shelf past the L's, then the O's and P's. I got to the Q's and crouched down to where they changed to R's, then followed the spines of the books with my finger.

Ra-, Re-, Ri-, Ro-, Roosevelt. There were five or six books on Franklin D. Roosevelt, but my finger traced back a little to the left and pulled out the one book the library had on his wife.

There was that smiling, big toothed woman again, not from Mr. Flynn's wall, but rather from Miss E.'s. The black and white photo of her filled the cover. Across the top, the title "Eleanor Roosevelt" and below that in smaller print "A Pictorial Biography". Even though he was President and she was only First Lady, I thought it a little unfair that FDR got a whole collection of books about him, and Eleanor didn't even get a complete book, just one filled mostly with pictures, like there wasn't enough to say about her. But at that moment, a pictorial biography was just fine with me, because I felt certain that I'd find the picture I was looking for. That picture of the two women standing side by side, smiling at each other in their hats.

I flipped through the pages, resisting the temptation to look at all the pictures and read the captions. I focused on finding the one I really needed, but I couldn't help but stop at a few that caught my eye. With Shirley Temple in 1938, at the United Nations in 1947 wearing headphones for translations, walking their dog Fala. Then I saw it.

The photo was on a page by itself, across from one of the few pages that actually had a paragraph of text. The two ladies in the photo practically jumped off the page at me I was so excited, and so nervous I had to blink my eyes a few times to get them to focus on the tiny print of the caption below.

"First Lady Eleanor Roosevelt in 1935 chatting with aviation pioneer Amelia Earhart."

Amelia Earhart! I actually smacked myself on the forehead. She should have been a gimme, maybe not as easy as Einstein or Lincoln, but definitely not a photo we should still be puzzling over months into Mr. Flynn's assignment. Even without the pictures, if asked to name 50 important American woman, certainly one of us would have come up with Amelia Earhart. But we were all so distracted by trying to match photos, we never slowed down enough to even come up with a list of possibilities or to consider who we might be looking for.

I put the Eleanor Roosevelt book back on the shelf, and hurried back toward the beginning of the biography section. I had a name for my mystery woman, but I wasn't satisfied that I had all the pieces to my puzzle yet. I thought again about how Miss E. would have ended up with an autographed photograph of Eleanor Roosevelt (from 1935 chatting with aviation pioneer Amelia Earhart, or so the pictorial biography told me), and why she had a wall covered with photos of a woman whom I now knew to be Amelia Earhart. I mean, she's got a pretty interesting story and all, but how exactly does one become an Amelia Earhart fan?

I found the E's and scanned for Earhart. One, two, three books on Amelia. She was two up on her pal Eleanor and they were real biographies with pages full of text, not just pictures. I pulled all three from the shelf and knew at once how Mr. Flynn had tricked us. One of us surely had looked at these books. We'd covered the whole biography section end to end, but the photos on the cover looked nothing like the one hanging on his wall. Two of the books used the same picture. The Amelia we knew and recognized, wearing her aviators cap with the flaps covering her ears and her mop of hair tucked neatly inside. In that picture she looked beautiful, perfect, not like a woman who actually flew planes, but more like a model in a studio who was made up to look like a woman who flew planes. The third book actually used a painting on the cover. Amelia was wearing a dress and had her hair done up stylishly. Neither image bore any resemblance to the smiling, squinty, tousle-haired woman in Mr. Flynn's room.

So I had figured out a few things that day. Whether I decided to tell the class about Amelia Earhart or enjoy the excitement on my own for a little while, I'd at least have a few tips to bring back to room 110.

1. Look for connections to other famous Americans. If Mr. Flynn's top one hundred weren't exactly A-list when it came to history-book history, they might at least have gotten a few pictures taken with an A-lister.
2. Come up with a list of likely suspects. We were searching all of American history for one hundred

matches. We needed to narrow our possibilities down to start coming up with a "Top Americans" list of our own. It took the searching method we'd been using and put it in reverse. Come up with the names first and then see if any of them matched the pictures.

3. Look beyond the iconic photos. It seemed like every famous person had that one photograph that everyone pictured when they thought of that person. These were the photos that got used on book covers, but Mr. Flynn had dug a little deeper into photographic history. If he could slip Amelia Earhart under our noses without us noticing, chances are there were a few more just like her up on the wall. We might just need to open all the books we'd already gone through and look beyond the covers.

I checked out all three of the Amelia Earhart books and got as far as a bench outside the library before stopping to flip through them. I was curious. I knew about her but I didn't really know about her. And something about the woman was interesting enough to prompt Miss E.'s collection of photographs. I figured at the very least, knowing more about her would give me a topic to chat with Miss E. about next time I was invited into her kitchen.

I started with the book that looked like it was written for elementary school students because I figured it would give me some quick information without a ton of reading. Sure enough, the first page listed some "Quick Facts".

- Born July 24, 1897 – disappeared July 2, 1937
- First woman to fly solo across the Atlantic
- Attempted to fly around the world

I flipped the page. Most of the quick facts I knew. A couple pages in, I learned that Amelia had been an advocate for women's rights and that she joined the faculty of Purdue University to counsel women on careers and help inspire others with her love for aviation—already pretty impressive for a woman who is mostly remembered for the flight she didn't complete. I read on and skimmed through an hour by hour description of her solo flight across the Atlantic. Some facts surprised me, like how Amelia didn't like the fit of the traditional aviation clothes so she started wearing the khaki slacks and jacket that became so recognizable, or how she didn't like coffee and drank tomato juice on all her long flights.

Most of the second half of the slim book focused on her last flight. There was a two-page map of her route, and a few grainy photos taken on the trip of her and her navigator, a man named Fred Noonan. Fred Noonan.

There's a feeling you get when you're getting close to finishing a puzzle, and the number of pieces left is small enough that you find their home right after picking them up. The puzzle's not done yet and you're not sure how the whole picture's going to end up looking, but you know you've got it solved and it's just a matter of picking up all the pieces and putting them where they belong. And that's how I suddenly felt sitting on that bench outside the library.

I flipped back a few pages to the beginning of the last chapter for information on the start of the world flight. Amelia left from Oakland, California in May of 1937. She was 40 years old the year she made that flight. I made a quick calculation in my head and decided that 40 plus 30 years equaled 70. I flipped toward the back of the book again to look more closely at one of those grainy photos of Amelia and Fred Noonan. A photo that I thought I might have seen before, except maybe the one I saw was autographed. I jumped toward the beginning of the book and read again about women's rights and tomato juice. And then I ended up back where I started, at the quick facts page and the last piece of the puzzle clicked into place.

Born July 24, 1897 – disappeared July 2, 1937

My guess is that any biography I pulled off the library shelves would have listed a "Born" date, and a "Died" date. Except for the one I held in my hands and the two others on the bench beside me. And of course the distinction made perfect sense. After all, no one really knew what happened to Amelia Earhart that day when she didn't show up at Howland Island. And certainly disappearing in the middle of the Pacific Ocean, you'd have to assume that someone was dead, even if you found no evidence.

So I'm sure the editor of that book thought that "disappeared" was the best word to describe what happened to Amelia Earhart on July 2, 1937. But if I'd walked back into the library and took a look at one of their big unabridged dictionaries, I would have found two subtly different definitions.

1. To cease to exist.
2. To pass out of sight; vanish.

The editor of the nice little Amelia Earhart biography for elementary school kids certainly meant the first definition, but what I'd realized when that last puzzle piece fit into its home and I got my first look at the complete picture, was that what Amelia Earhart had actually done was the second definition.

Because when someone disappears, all it really means is that you can't see them anymore. So I thought while I sat on that bench and the world walked by around me, that Amelia Earhart could be dead at the bottom of some ocean or on some deserted island. Or, she could be growing old on a farm not too far away from the spot where she started her flight, drinking tomato juice, looking at autographed pictures of Fred Noonan and Eleanor Roosevelt hanging on her wall, and chatting with the local grocery delivery girl about women's rights.

There was no way I was telling this secret. Room 110 would have to wait to find out who the mystery woman on the wall was. I was holding three books in my hands that described how her life ended out near some tiny island in the Pacific Ocean, but I knew that come Wednesday of next week, I'd be delivering a box of groceries to Amelia Earhart.

Questions

The six-day wait was unbearable. Each day in history, I stole glances at the Amelia Earhart photograph. There was no doubt in my mind that it was Miss E. Her hair was shorter now and gray of course, but I could still recognize the curly windblown mop that it once was. The thing that sealed the deal though was her eyes. They were the same thirty years later, still squinting like she was looking for something on a sunset horizon.

What I wasn't sure of was why a world famous aviator, women's rights advocate, and university faculty member would choose to disappear after nearly completing a flight around the world and then hide out in the middle of nowhere for thirty years.

When I wasn't daydreaming in school or delivering groceries, I busied myself with reading the other two biographies. They both contained pretty much the same information, but I still read them both cover to cover. I learned about her childhood and had a good laugh picturing Miss E. rumbling down the makeshift wooden ramp she'd built in her backyard when she was denied a ride on a roller coaster at the World's Fair. I read about her early days of flying, when keeping an airplane in the air was mostly about luck and fearlessness, and I learned the details of her many record breaking flights, not just the Atlantic crossing and the world flight, but her other firsts – Hawaii to California, California to Mexico, Mexico to New York, and her various cross country speed records.

With each new fact, I couldn't help but wonder why most people only knew about the last event in her life. It seemed to me that Amelia Earhart put more into the first forty years of her life than most people put into eighty or ninety, which added to the puzzle. Why call it all off at forty? She had a husband, a successful career, and was doing something she'd yearned to do since childhood – fly. My fifteen year old brain couldn't wrap itself around what could be missing from her life that would prompt her to ditch it all for a farm in nowhere California. As I biked from school to Johnson's Wednesday afternoon, I was determined to find out.

I tumbled into the store and eagerly looked around for the delivery box.

"Nothing today Elizabeth," Mr. Johnson said from behind the counter. "Go enjoy the afternoon. Looks like you've got the day off."

I stood puzzled for a moment, questions half formed in my mouth until I finally got the words out. "What about Miss E.? She's a Wednesday delivery."

"Not this week. She didn't call and order anything for today." He lifted his paper, signaling that the conversation was over and leaving me to read the front page headline for an article on the antiwar movement that was gathering steam in San Francisco.

I dragged myself outside and made it to a bench near the bulletin board. The excitement that had built up over the last week was emptying onto the sidewalk. Why would she stop her grocery delivery? Was she just going back to her old habit or did she not want to see me? Had she found out that I'd learned her secret or was she concerned I would figure things out if she allowed me to keep visiting?

The excitement that had left me was gradually being replaced with anger. She was messing with me. First, she started having her groceries delivered so I had to go out to her farm. She left the envelope like she was some hermit who couldn't even greet me at the door to pay for her stuff. Then she had me into her house like she was inviting me into some secret Amelia Earhart shrine, only to cut things off the next week. At fifteen, I hadn't had a real boyfriend yet, but if I had, I would have compared the whole thing to a breakup. And if it were a breakup, there would have been an angry note stuck in a locker door demanding an explanation. I decided to do the next best thing.

I tossed my backpack in my basket and hopped on my bike. I pedaled the miles out to Miss E.'s farm easily now. The months of delivering had really gotten me in shape and the ride that took me the better part of the afternoon I could now do in what felt like minutes.

The farm was quiet as usual when I got there, but the red pickup was parked in front of the house. When I saw it, a thought came to me that I hadn't had before, and for a moment I was concerned. What if something had happened to Miss E.? She lived out here all by herself and could be sick or hurt. But when I reached the door, I heard the familiar music and could see movement inside the dim living room.

I rapped on the screen door hard enough to bounce it in its frame, but I wanted to be sure she heard me. I didn't wait for a reply. I pulled the three library books out of my backpack and dropped them on the porch in front of the door.

"Chew on that, Meelie," I mumbled as I stomped back to my bike.

Answers

There was an order for groceries the following Wednesday. I arrived at the house half expecting there to be another envelope on the screen door, and was relieved when there wasn't. I knocked and heard Miss E.'s voice calling from the kitchen. I walked past the photographs again, scanning the wall for ones I now recognized from the books I'd read.

Miss E. was seated at the kitchen table just as she had been two weeks earlier. This time though, there were two mugs of tomato juice, and my three library books sat in a neat stack between them.

"Looks like these are due next week, Bets. Best take them back so you don't get any fines." I set the box down on the kitchen cupboard and slid cautiously into a chair when Miss E. gestured toward it. Like the envelope that wasn't on the door, I was expecting a confrontation that didn't come. My head was full of questions again, but Miss E. started talking and didn't stop for a long time, so I just listened and kept my mouth shut (except for the times that it hung open in surprise).

"There's a long story to be told here, Bets. So make yourself comfortable and drink your tomato juice," she started and then paused until I pulled the mug closer to me and took a tentative sip. "Starts way back when I made my first Atlantic crossing. I wasn't even flying the plane then, just a passenger, but everyone was paying attention because I was the first woman ever to do it. Seems funny now, like giving the spotlight to the first woman to ride a bus or a taxi cab."

I must have reacted to her using the word spotlight, thinking of how hard I tried to avoid attention at school, because she noticed it and raised an eyebrow. "Well, when I got off that plane there was a mighty big spotlight," she continued. "And I wasn't expecting it. I only made the flight because I was excited about the adventure, and I figured afterwards I'd go back to my life, the same as it was before. But once I stepped onto the ground in England, everything changed. Should have figured it with the newspaper connections George Putnam had, but I didn't.

"Funny thing about a spotlight though. Once you're in it, you start to forget what things were like before. You get used to the attention, and you start thinking about things you can do to keep that attention. Don't get me wrong, Bets. I'm a flyer. Any flight I made I did because I simply loved being in the air, but talking to reporters before I left and smiling for photographers once I was back on the ground started to feel like that was part of flying too.

"Well, I guess I liked the attention enough to marry a publicist. And sometimes a spotlight can be put to good use. With so many people paying attention to me for the flying I did, I had a good stage for talking about some of the other things that were important to me. But the spotlight gets tiresome after too long... so do publicist husbands."

I must have looked surprised at the remark, but Miss E. put a hand up to stop my reaction. "Come on, Bets. You read those books so you must know something about that marriage. George Putnam was a good man and he adored me, but women who want to settle down to a domestic life in their husband's home don't usually spend their married years crisscrossing the globe on solo flights.

"Anyone on the outside must have figured George and I had a pretty good life. Beautiful home, showing up at fancy parties, driving around in shiny cars. But I had enough of it all, enough of George, and enough of the spotlight.

"So a flight around the world seemed like a pretty good idea. Sure, I agreed to write about it, and George was sitting back home eagerly awaiting any dispatches I sent him. I knew there'd be a big crowd waiting for me back in Oakland, but look at a map of my route and you'll find lots of out of the way places where sometimes the welcome wagon was just a few men waiting to fill the tanks and check the flaps.

"I guess I was hoping for something different when I returned. I hinted to a reporter that I'd be done with long distance flying. Stunt flying they still called it back then. Made him promise not to write a word of it until I was close to finishing the flight. But I knew things wouldn't change just because I wanted them to.

"Had an old friend in California. Name was Sam Casey. Well, more than an old friend, I suppose. There were other romances before George of course, and Sam was one of them. Sam was a sailor and spent most of his time on a ship in the Pacific while the navy kept an eye on Japan. We weren't at war yet in '37, but with Japan and Germany flexing their muscles, we knew that's where we were headed.

"I'd stayed in touch with Sam after I married. A letter now and then or a visit when I was in California and he was on leave. It was harmless, Bets. George knew all about it and didn't trouble himself over it. He certainly wasn't going to stop a grown woman from seeing an old friend.

"It was Sam who put the idea in my head. This farm was his, and he'd joke sometimes about me taking a wrong turn on one of my flights and landing here. Landing here, away from the crowds and the spotlight.

"I didn't plan to slip away, not at first. But the farther I flew away from my life back home, the more the idea wound into my thoughts. Flying seems like a whole lot of doing nothing sometimes, Bets. Oh, there's the takeoff and landing, but between them, you're just pointing your plane in a straight line and looking out ahead at the horizon. There's lots of time to think, and I found myself thinking more and more about Sam Casey's farm."

Miss E. paused for a long time. I sipped my tomato juice uncomfortably waiting for her to start again, not knowing if I should say something or if she'd reached the end of the story and I just hadn't figured it out. Finally, she let out a long sigh and started talking.

"I realized wanting to run away from the spotlight was only half of it, Bets. And it's the worse half. It wasn't until I was almost done with my world flight before I figured out what I wanted to run to. I got word to Sam what I was thinking, and he started preparing for my arrival on this farm while folks down in Oakland were gearing up for the same. All that was left was to convince my navigator, because if I was going to disappear I certainly couldn't have Fred Noonan showing up at the airport. I thought I'd have a hard time of it, but Fred took to the idea right away. Fred had bounced around a lot, worked for Pan Am for a spell but left when he felt like they weren't paying him enough. He'd divorced not long before the flight, so picking up and putting down roots someplace new had an appeal to him as well.

"I won't bore you with geography or the how to of things, Bets. I'll just say that the Pacific's a mighty big place, and it's easy to get lost if a person wants to. They were looking for us on one tiny speck of an island, and we flew to another, and another, and another. Wasn't any trouble landing here without being seen. Map was different back then. Not as many people, only a few farms, town was not much more than a place where two roads bumped together. By the time the ships stopped searching the ocean for me, I was sitting cozily on this farm."

She must have seen the discomfort on my face. "I don't take it lightly what I did. I can talk about it easier now, thirty years later. But there were lots of nights I cried myself to sleep thinking I'd done the wrong thing and wondering if there was a way I could undo it. Fooling the whole world might feel like a fun thing to think about, but actually doing it's another story. And playing dead for a husband. Well, how do you undo that? George was always going to love me more than I was going to love him, and maybe he was better off without me in the end. I was only part wife for him anyway, the rest of me was just someone for him to publish and promote. But I left friends and family, and a home, and a life too. You've seen all I've got left of that hanging on the wall in my hallway. That was the hardest part."

There was another long pause. This time I didn't sit there wondering if the story was done. Because I knew it wasn't, and I had the sinking feeling that the worst was yet to come. Miss E. sat for a while and sipped her tomato juice a few times. I tried to picture her flying her airplane with a thermos full of tomato juice on the seat next to her, and I imagined her reaching for it without looking, like my father reaches for his coffee while he's reading the paper.

"Your father's in Vietnam, Bets?" Her question brought me back from my daydream and reminded me that there was a world outside Miss E.'s kitchen. I opened my mouth to answer, but felt like it still wasn't my turn to speak and just nodded instead.

"Wars. We keep having them even though it seems like while we're in one, all we want to do is get out of it. We don't ever learn our lesson though.

"I settled in on Sam's farm, but most of the time I was here on my own. A letter would come now and then and there were times he was home on leave. We'd stay here mostly. We didn't dare go anywhere we'd see too many people for fear someone would recognize me, but we'd take lots of drives on roads that wouldn't show up on most maps, and if you've got to stay in one place, a farm's just about the best place to do it.

"It was those times that Sam was here when I was happiest. He became a best friend. Well, with me mostly hiding away, he was the only one I had, but still the best I could have ever hoped for. With Sam, talking and laughing were easy, and there was never anything more important than the moment we were in and the place where we were. That's just about all anyone could ask for in a friend. The times in between, the times when he was gone, that's when I couldn't help but think about the decision I'd made, wondering if it was the right one, and feeling the dread of knowing that there was no going back.

"Well Bets, you've read enough of your history book to know that things went from bad to worse with Japan in the Pacific, and before too long everyone in a uniform was shipping out. So we were back to just letters again, some from islands I'd flown to. Then the letters stopped. Of course you hope at first that it's just the mail. You tell yourself that ships can take weeks to get into a port with mail service. But then one day, a shiny black car came down the road and I knew before it even stopped in front of the house. I wasn't a military wife so there was no officer coming to give me his sympathy and a folded up flag. Instead a lawyer came up to the door with a briefcase full of papers."

There was a quick quiver in her voice. Damp eyes were brushed dry and I thought for a second that the emotion in Miss. E's story would start to flow from her, but then she turned it off like flipping a switch. And in that brief second, she reminded me of my mother.

"Well, Sam was gone and that was that. Killed in some battle near Saipan. Military doesn't send condolence letters to women who are just hiding out on soldiers' farms instead of being married to them. But Sam had written a will before he left and the farm went to me, legal signed and sealed. He didn't have any other close family, so I suppose if he hadn't put things down in writing everything would have gone to the state and I would have been looking for a place to park my plane."

I was slumped down in my chair still sorting through the story she'd just told me. I was exhausted, and I imagine Miss E. felt the same, but I knew I had to listen to the end.

"Where could I go? George had already remarried, and I wouldn't have gone back to him even if he wasn't. Would he have wanted me? The world had moved on too. War had come and gone, and people were going someplace new. What did they need with a woman pilot from a decade ago? And how could I just reappear, explaining why I'd done what I'd done.

"So I just planted myself on this farm. I didn't get what I wanted, but I at least got rid of what I didn't want. No spotlight out here, huh Bets?" She smiled a little, then stood up and took her mug to the sink, her tomato juice apparently finished along with her story. "So here I am."

I let it all sink in. I looked at the books on the table and thought about the person they described, and then the person in front of me with a story that would rewrite everything that was in all the books. It was the kind of story that would make for a scandalous magazine headline, until you had a chance to sit down in that person's kitchen, drink some tomato juice with her, and hear her side of it.

When I finally found my voice, I only had one question left. "Where's the plane?"

Electra

Miss E. grabbed the handle of the door on the left and put her weight into pulling it. I realized I should help her, but before I had the chance the heavy wooden door slid open on the rusty rollers above and Miss E. was already pushing the other one open.

The scene inside was so different from the sunlit world around me that it was like looking into an old photograph. The barn was absolute stillness, all the colors muted browns and yellows. Hay dust hung in the air, caught in the shafts of sunlight that snuck through the cracks in the barn siding. The stalls all stood empty, but they looked just as they would have the last time the barn held animals. Piles of hay lay in the corners, ropes and feed bags still hung on hooks. A tractor hulked far back in the barn, and a plow beside it waited to be pulled through the fields.

The plane stood in the middle of the large space looking both out of place and perfectly natural at the same time. It had no business being there among the animal stalls and farm equipment, yet everything in the scene seemed to be from the same time, as if the door was shut in 1937 and was just now being opened again.

Miss E. paused in the doorway for a moment looking at the plane. She walked toward it, turning briefly to look at me in a way that gave me permission to follow. I stepped through the doorway and was hit by a wall of heat and the smell of hay, like the air too had been trapped in the barn for years. Miss E. walked around the plane, and I followed at a distance. She touched parts of it as she came close, a wingtip, the underside of the tail, a propeller blade. I dared not, but my eyes took it all in. She grasped the edge of a wing flap and moved it up and down with a satisfied nod. Watching her inspect her plane, I could imagine her in some faraway place, South America or Africa, getting ready to fly to her next destination.

The plane was old with the abuse of many miles, the metal surrounding the engines blackened by heat and oil, the skin scratched and worn, and the seams filled with the dust of endless airfields. But if it looked any other way it would have seemed wrong. If it were shiny and new, I would have been disappointed. Here was the plane that had been lost at sea or on some deserted island, so everybody thought. Here it was after all these years. Why shouldn't it look like it had been around the world and back again? It had.

"Not in a museum," Miss E.'s voice interrupted my thoughts, "Don't have to just stand there looking." I turned to see her opening a door in the side of the plane and ducking her head as she crawled in. I followed, putting my hands on either side of the door and pulling myself through it. Like the barn, the inside of the plane looked as if it hadn't been touched in thirty years. We squeezed between the large tanks of fuel – I knew from reading the Amelia Earhart books that they had been installed to increase the plane's range – and eventually came to the cockpit. Miss E. slid easily into the seat on the left, but I hesitated, wanting to soak it all in: the small space packed with gauges, switches, and levers; the windows offering a cropped view of the world beyond, and the low curve just above my head. I grumbled about a ride in the back seat of our car, yet Miss E. had flown around the world in this tiny space.

She patted the seat beside her and I wiggled in. Once there, I felt more at ease. The old leather seat was worn and soft. My legs and feet fit neatly under the control panel, and my new position offered me more headroom and a better view out the windows.

"Do you," I hesitated, "Do you ever fly it?" After I spoke, I wished I could pull the words back into my mouth. Something about sitting in a plane that had been lost to the world for thirty years made me feel like it wasn't my place to speak and I should be a silent observer – like sitting at the grownup table during a fancy dinner.

But Miss E. only smiled. "You ever hear a Lockheed Electra during takeoff?" she said. I shrugged my shoulders and shook my head at the same time. "Those two Wasp engines were designed before anyone thought up the idea of noise pollution. Half the county would be looking out their windows and stepping into their front yards, trying to figure out what was making all the noise, and then they'd be craning their necks to watch it fly over, looking like no plane they've ever seen. Before I got five hundred feet off the ground, the controllers at the airport would see me with their fancy radar screens. They'd radio to me asking for a flight plan while they jabbered to themselves trying to figure out how an airplane just appeared out of the middle of the corn fields. Next they'd be looking for my transponder signal, which they wouldn't find."

I must have looked confused because Miss E paused and raised her eyebrows in a questioning way.

"Transponder? It's a special radio that every plane these days needs to have. All the while you're in the air, it's sending out your identification, what direction you're going, and how fast, so the controllers in the tower and the other planes around know what you're up to and everyone can stay out of everyone else's way. But the Electra was made long before transponders, so they'd have an unidentified aircraft and that would really get their dander up. They'd watch me on radar and wherever I landed there'd be a welcome wagon. By the time the evening news came on the TV's, everyone would be talking about the old lady who climbed out of that antique aircraft. And gosh don't that plane look just like the one that Earhart woman flew? And what year was that? And, how old would she be today?"

We sat in silence for a moment while Miss E.'s words sunk in. My eyes scanned the gauges and controls in the plane and then moved up toward the windows. I looked out again through them to the scene beyond, and the barn door seemed smaller than ever, as if the plane's wings would hit the sides before it ever made it out the opening.

"So you're stuck here?" I finally said.

"Yep, I suppose I am. The plane's stuck here least ways, and I'm not really going anywhere without it." Miss E. let out a sigh and then sat staring out the windows. I let her sit in silence, and then she spoke again. "This barn and that field have been here long before they built the airport, so I suppose it's just coincidence. Coincidence that I ended up here too. But sittin' here in this barn, looking out those doors at the field beyond, that long field. Never saw a field so flat. I remember landing on it when I came here, so smooth I thought I was on pavement. It'd be perfect. And it all lines up with the runway at Oakland just fifty miles away. Took off from there thirty years ago, and it just sits out there every day so close I could hit it with a thrown stone."

Another long pause, long enough that I had a question on my lips when Miss E started speaking again.

"Around the world minus fifty miles. I come out here and I sit and look out at the last miles of my world flight – fifty miles just waiting to be flown. Be an easy flight, 'specially with things all lined up so nicely. We'd get out to the end of the field rising above those trees, and we'd see the city, wouldn't be but a few minutes and we'd see those fancy airstrip lights they have out there now. This Electra could practically do a flight like that by herself."

I felt the gravity of what Miss E. was saying weigh down the cockpit, and the excitement of being in the plane started to sour when I realized what it meant to her. To me, the plane was a discovered treasure and a thrilling secret, something the world thought was lost, that I had found. To Miss E. it was an unfinished goal, a reminder of a journey and a life that hadn't turned out as planned.

Without warning, one of the plane's engines thundered to life, and I turned to see Miss E.'s hand on a switch. She flipped another switch and the second engine coughed twice and then roared.

"What are you doing?" I shouted, and she said something back, but I could hear nothing over the sound of the engines. Miss E. scanned the gauges and then started working the controls. I could see her feet moving the rudder pedals on the floor and her hands push the yoke away from her and then pull it back again. She looked out the side windows at the flaps on the wings and then watched them move up and down as she turned the yoke side to side.

She sat back in the seat comfortably, but her eyes were focused on the horizon. Her hands held the yoke lightly, not moving it much, as if she were keeping the plane level and flying a steady course. I sat watching her face and when she smiled, she became Amelia Earhart. She wasn't wearing the funny hat with the goggles, or the jacket with the fur lined collar that everyone would recognize from the magazine pictures, but if I held up the picture hanging in my history classroom next to Miss E. at that moment, they would have been twins. The smile seemed to change her whole face, made her eyes twinkle and her hair curl. Now the sour face she wore into town made sense, because the moment Miss E. smiled like that at anyone, they would have rushed off for sure, shouting that they'd just seen Amelia Earhart.

The roar of the engines grew and I looked down to see Miss E.'s right hand moving a lever that I figured was the throttle. She moved it back and forth and the engines revved up and then fell back to an idle. Each time she seemed to let the engines rev a little longer until she took her hand off the throttle and let them continue to run at that high speed. The plane shuddered with the engines' energy and the very air around us seemed to vibrate. Their sound filled the cockpit, until there was nothing else, and I gripped the seat beneath me, sure that any second we would spring from the ground in a tremendous leap. It was simply impossible to imagine that much power sitting motionless in the barn. And then, they stopped.

The propellers still spun blurred circles, and the engines coughed, the one on my side sputtering to life again for a second before the fuel in the pistons was used up. Then it was silent. I stared at Miss E., eyes wide, mouth open, my initial surprise at the engines starting now turned to wonderment that we were still on the ground. The smile was gone from her face, and she was slumped back in her seat, her gaze still out the windows but in a dreamy way, the intensity gone, not like she was living it, but only wishing it.

I couldn't help but break the silence. "What happened?" I half shouted still compensating for the now silent engines. My voice brought Miss E. back to the cockpit, and she raised her eyebrows in a question. "The engines. You started them up. I thought... Well, you said... about the airport. I thought we were..."

Miss E. straightened up and her expression returned to normal. "Got to turn these old engines over every month or so. Leave them just sitting here and they'll seize. Won't ever start again if that happens. I suppose people are about the same way, huh Bets?" She pulled herself from the seat and disappeared into the back of the plane.

She followed her path in reverse, circling the plane, touching parts of it, and then leaving it to close the barn doors. I stood in the now too bright sunlight and once again let Miss E. struggle with the doors rather than helping her. I could do nothing but watch the image of the plane in the barn slowly get shut inside. One door closed and then the other until there was just a sliver of light getting through, one beam falling on the metal skin of the plane, and then nothing.

"Well, you've seen my Electra," Miss E. sighed and snapped closed the lock on the doors. She walked off toward the house, and I knew it wasn't my place to follow. I stood where I was for a minute more, watching her leave and letting all she'd told me and all I'd seen sink in.

On my ride home my mind kept going back to what Miss E. had said about those engines and how they needed to be started every month or so. Thirty years is a long time to take care of engines that you know won't ever really be used again. I thought about how Miss E. looked sitting in that cockpit with those engines running like that, and I was certain she didn't even know I was there. She wasn't revving those engines and working the controls so I could see what the plane could do, she was doing it because every month for the last thirty years she'd gone out to that barn and dreamed of flying that plane again. And I thought about how the plane was stuck there – a treasure, but at the same time a secret that had to be hidden away, one taking the shine off the other. Because after all, what good is a treasure if you can't ever show it to anyone, or tell anyone about it, or let it fly through the air like it was meant to do.

Perspective

After meeting the long lost Amelia Earhart and seeing her airplane hidden away in a barn for thirty years instead of being at the bottom of the Pacific Ocean somewhere, most people would think that their lives would change somehow, that knowing a famous person and being let in on an amazing secret would rub off on them and make them famous or amazing too. Those people would be wrong.

The day after I sat down in Amelia Earhart's kitchen, heard her story, and climbed into her Electra to watch her warm up its engines, I pretty much did what I did any other Thursday. And thinking about being in the Electra with its engines roaring, while the three books the Forestville library had on the subject were sitting on Amelia Earhart's kitchen table, well that was a little distracting during classes, but I was still in my classes. I still rode my bike to school and delivered groceries that afternoon. No one came knocking at my door for an interview or stopped me on the street for my autograph. I still had homework to do and my mother was still unemotional and uninvolved.

I didn't tell anyone in history class that I had figured out the Amelia Earhart photograph. We still had about thirty to name, so adding one more to our list wouldn't get us the prize. But mostly, she still felt like a secret, and me knowing who the photograph was seemed a part of that. Sure, I could say I figured it out and not tell everyone that I had actually met her, but for me, knowing who the person in the photograph was and actually meeting the person were all rolled into one. Besides, if I figured out the photograph, I'd also have to write about her importance in twenty words or less. "Amelia Earhart lives on a farm outside Forestville, California where she is hiding her plane in a barn." Eighteen. Two to spare. "She's alive!" Do contractions count as one word or two?

I thought about riding my bike out to Miss E.'s farm. My last trip there certainly went beyond just delivering groceries, so I didn't really need to wait until another delivery day, but something made me feel like time needed to pass. After all, thirty years was a long time to go without telling anyone your story. Miss E. was likely not interested in a follow up interview.

I dared to hope for another chance to sit in her plane again, and at the same time wondered if I'd even get a seat at the kitchen table again. I replayed the day, concerned that I'd gone too far in asking to see her plane or that Miss E. had let me too far into her story and would decide instead to shut me out.

But all I could do was wait. I went to school, I delivered groceries, and I hung out with Cassie, Anne, and Susan on the weekend. The only thing that happened of any significance was a letter from my father that arrived on Saturday. He wrote regularly, but regular for my father was not often. That was OK. Not much of my father came through in his letters. Just like talking to him when we were sitting in the same room, what he said was only a small part of what he communicated. How he stood or sat, his expressions and gestures, what words he said quietly, or quickly, or slowly, and what words he didn't say.

None of that came through in the letters, yet my mother still folded them carefully after she'd read them aloud to me, and then she'd walk off with them. To put them somewhere I guess. I didn't think she'd just throw them out, but I never saw them again. Part of me wondered if she was really reading what was on the page, or if she was filtering and putting her own twist on my father's words. I wondered, but wasn't about to go snooping in my mother's dresser drawers for my father's letters.

But I missed him. All the time. Like the refrain that ran through my head in the weeks before my father left, my father now being gone was a thought that worked its tendrils into every part of my day. When I rode my bike to school or out on deliveries, I thought of my father and the day he gave me the bike. A good grade on a test only forced me to remember that he wouldn't be home that evening for me to proudly show it to him. I had a drawer full of tests and essays waiting for him when he returned. School and friends and Mr. Flynn's pictures were small distractions.

Miss E. and her Electra were bigger ones, but even they couldn't push thoughts of my father entirely from my mind. When Wednesday finally rolled around again and I was boxing Miss E.'s groceries for delivery, it felt like any other delivery day. But I didn't want it to be. I had a sinking feeling that I would arrive at her door only to find another envelope and no invitation to come in. Or if I was invited in that there would only be awkward conversation, like running into a boy outside a classroom after a first date gone wrong.

As I pedaled out to the dirt road and turned onto it heading for her farm, I rehearsed conversations in my head – what I might ask her and what she might answer. I tried out several, to make sure I was ready for anything, but I had no way of planning for what was to come.

There was no envelope stuck in the screen door, so I knocked and felt comfortable enough to open the door and walk in before I heard her reply. There was movement back in the kitchen, so I just walked back and found Miss E. in the kitchen pouring two mugs of tomato juice.

"Good to have you here again, Bets. Wasn't quite sure if you were going to show up at my doorstep again the very next day, or if I was never going to see you again. But you got it just right, huh?" I smiled and shrugged and put the box of groceries down on the countertop, satisfied that my week of patiently waiting and wondering had been acknowledged. "Help yourself to a chair," she said as she sat down and placed the two mugs on the table. "Looking forward to hearing your story."

I hesitated until the silence in the room became uncomfortable. "My... my what?"

"Well, c'mon, Bets. I've already decided you're the most interesting person in town. Always palling around with a group of girls for ice cream or pizza, riding your bike wherever you go, and knocking out the school's pain in the shorts with one punch. I suppose Forestville hasn't seen anything like you since..." She paused and smiled. "Well, since I came to town I guess."

I thought about what she was asking for, and then said quickly, "I don't have a story."

"Oh, Bets. Don't be silly. Everyone's got a story. It just doesn't seem like a story to you because it's your day to day and you're living it."

I thought about that. And I thought about all the talking Miss E. had done the week before. She told me a story that would rival anything that was in the Forestville library, but to her is was just something that happened in life. I thought about my dad ... and my mother. And then I started talking. I talked for a long time, longer than I thought possible. Long enough to finish my tomato juice and have Miss E. pour seconds. I told Miss E. about the last few places we'd lived, but not because those places were really important to me, just because they'd give her an idea of my moving around from place to place. I told her about my father in Vietnam, and my mother. My mother who seemed unchanged through it all, unemotional, unresponsive. But I didn't say that. Instead I told her in a cheerful voice how my mom was making the time without my father easier by telling stories about him at the dinner table.

She just sat still through most of what I said, nodding a couple times and sipping her juice. But when I talked about my mother she gave a quick "mm-hmm" like she was only half listening. I wasn't sure how much eye contact I was making through the first part of my story, but I realized I was having trouble looking Miss E. in the eye when I talked about my mother.

Finally she stopped my monologue by standing up and taking our mugs to the sink. "I've got a feeling you're giving me half a story, Bets. You sure that's how things are between you and your mother?"

I shrugged my reply.

"Well Bets, it seems to me like you need a change of perspective." I said nothing, only looked at her with confusion on my face and waited for her to explain. "You have anything taking up your time this weekend other than visits to the pizza place and the ice cream parlor?" she asked, and I shook my head. "Good then. Come on over here Saturday morning and we'll see what we can do about your perspective."

I protested a little and tried to ask her questions about what she meant, but she cut me off and before I knew it I was on the front porch with the screen door slapping closed behind me. I dreaded the weekend. I was certain that Miss E. knew what I'd said about my mother was a lie, and come Saturday I would be lectured on respect for adults and how parents are always right. At one point, I broke out in a cold sweat when it occurred to me that Miss. E could actually invite my mother out to her farm and I would be confronted by both of them when I entered the house. But what I found on Saturday morning was completely unexpected.

When I coasted my bike into the driveway Saturday morning, Miss E. was coming out of the house with a basket. She put it in the back of the red pickup and then turned to greet me.

"Good to see you, Bets. Didn't tell you what time, but you got it just right, huh?" I shrugged and smiled as if to say that I did indeed get it just right, but that I didn't really mean to and felt a little uncomfortable being complimented for it. My father would have understood all of that. "Well, Bets, sometimes things happen just right and we might as well take credit for them." Apparently, my father and Miss E. spoke the same language.

I was expecting a long conversation at the kitchen table, so I was surprised when Miss E opened the pickup door and climbed in. The window was already rolled down and she called through it. "Come on, Bets. Stop wasting the day, and get in." Still trying to figure out why we weren't going into the house for the lecture I'd been expecting, I leaned my bike on the kickstand and climbed into the pickup next to Miss E.

No small part of me was relieved that I did not go back in time. I had looked Miss E. in the eye, I had gone into her house, and now I was sitting in her pickup. Despite the eerie feeling I'd had when I saw them the first time, neither person, house, nor pickup had the ability to time travel after all.

I think maybe because the driver was as old as the truck, I'd assumed we'd be taking a slow drive, with careful turns, and long pauses at stop signs. I was quickly reminded that the woman beside me in the driver's seat flew airplanes cross-country at a time when most people had never even seen one. I'm not sure Miss E. would have passed a driving exam with her loose observance of the speed limit and the number of stop signs she rolled through, but once we were out on open country roads, her driving made the pickup seem like it was on autopilot while we chatted and enjoyed the scenery.

We drove long enough that I'd lost track of time. I hadn't really explored very far outside of Forestville. I could only ride so far on my bike, and my mother never really went anywhere, so I had a very limited mental map of the area. We went through a couple places that I guess were small towns, but anyone who didn't live there would probably drive right through without knowing it. Mostly there was a lot of open country, and only a couple of the roads we drove on were paved.

We turned off one of the paved roads when we passed a sign with an airplane on it, and then bounced along on a rutted dirt lane for a few minutes before we pulled into an open field with a few airplanes clustered around a small building. With a sinking stomach, I realized what Miss E. could mean by a change of perspective.

We got out of the pickup and Miss E. grabbed the basket from the back of the truck. We walked toward the cluster of planes, and I noticed for the first time a man, perched on a ladder and leaning most of his body into the engine of the plane parked closest to the building.

"Morning, Fred. Going to take the duster up this morning if that's OK."

The man pulled his head out of the engine compartment and his body seemed to unfold itself as he stepped to the ground. He pushed the hat back on his head to reveal a smiling face. "Sure, Meellie. She's gassed up and ready to go, although I don't have any dusting to do today."

"No matter. Just going to take my young friend for a look-see above the clouds," Miss E. said gesturing toward me. The man acknowledged what she'd said with a quick nod and then disappeared back into the engine he was working on.

My mind raced with the information it had been given. His name, his face, what I'd read in the Amelia Earhart books, and what Miss E. had told me. The conclusion was simple. Fred Noonan. "Fred Noonan?" I said it out loud.

"Quiet," Miss E. snapped. "Not right to talk about someone while they're still close enough to hear." She seemed to wait a few steps before continuing. "That's Fred alright. He had to go somewhere after we returned from our flight, and he picked here. There was no getting away from flying for Fred. For me neither, I suppose. He came here to manage this airfield, and he keeps busy with some crop dusting jobs and some small cargo flights when someone needs something to go someplace else in a hurry. He lets me fly the duster on some of the jobs and sometimes just for fun."

Since we were walking toward it, I figured that the red plane with a double set of wings parked to the side of the building was the duster. What showed of the motor looked old and greasy and the wings seemed to sag under their own weight. There were spots of new paint, as if holes in the skin of the plane had been patched and painted over carelessly. I had never been on a plane before. My father had of course, and he worked on planes all the time. I always figured I would have the chance to fly eventually, but I didn't expect it to be in an open cockpit plane that looked like it would never get off the ground.

Miss E must have read my mind. "Oh, the duster doesn't look like much, but it's a good plane. Never had a bad scare with it yet, and don't expect to." I raised my eyebrows wondering what the difference between a scare and a bad scare was, but Miss E. had already turned her back on me to climb into the plane. She lifted a foot and hopped up on the wing with an ease that surprised me. Before I knew it, she was seated in the plane and looking at me expectantly.

I stammered, searching for a reason not to get into the plane. "I... well, my mother... I guess. Well, I don't think my mother would want me to," I said finally deciding that using my mother as an excuse was my best bet.

"Bets, you and I both know your mother won't be finding out about this. We also know that you wouldn't let your mother stop you from something you wanted to do.

Climb on in." Admitting defeat, I struggled to pull myself onto the wing, and then carefully inched along until I could grasp the edge of the cockpit and pull myself toward it.

My next concern was that Miss E. had made herself at home in the rear seat, leaving the front seat for me. The worry must have shown on my face. "Don't worry yourself, Bets. I'll be steering from back here, you can sit yourself up there and enjoy the view." With that, I took a deep breath and climbed in.

I thought the Electra was loud. The duster took the prize. The engine coughed twice and the propeller turned slowly. Then it roared to life, turning the blades in front of me into a blur. The seat below me shook, my teeth vibrated, and holding onto the edges of the cockpit only sent the vibrations up my arms.

There were a few dials in front of me, duplicates of what Miss E. had behind I figured. I couldn't imagine how they did her much good though, since the needles bounced furiously and I had to squint to read them. There was a control stick between my legs as well, also a duplicate of Miss E's. That seemed to be the only thing in the plane that wasn't jumping up and down, only tilting slightly side to side as the plane made a turn here and there on the way out to the runway. Knowing that Miss E. had a firm hand at the controls was enough to allow me a small breath of relief.

The duster made a quick turn and then slowed to a stop, although the engine still made the air thick with noise. I figured we'd reached the runway and Miss E. was pointing the plane toward the other end. My view out the front was only sky since the duster's tail dragged low to the ground on a single small wheel and the taller front wheels under the wings pointed the nose far above the horizon. I could only crane my neck to see out the sides and behind.

"Ready, Bets?" Miss E.'s voice shouted behind me, almost lost in the roar of the engine. I didn't think I could manage a voice loud enough to be heard and instead meekly raised my hand in a thumbs up gesture. The engine couldn't possibly get louder, and then it did. I noticed a knob on the panel in front of me move as if it were being pulled out by an invisible hand, and I realized it was mirroring Miss E.'s as she pulled out her throttle and turned the low grumbling roar into a high pitched whine.

At first the duster stood still, reminding me of the Electra trapped back in the barn, and then we slowly began to roll forward again. Faster and faster, until the blur of fields outside the cockpit matched the whine of the engine. The plane tilted forward as the small tail wheel lifted off the ground and the view suddenly opened up in front of me. The small building and other planes were ahead of us, but we approached them so quickly, almost as soon as I'd noticed them, we were passing by them and leaving them behind.

The big front wheels were bumping along the grass runway, and then they weren't. Just like that we were in the air. And just as quickly the engine quieted and the vibrations stopped, as if the duster had been working with all its might to move along the ground at such a speed, and now that it was in the air and back in its element it could relax.

My eyes couldn't look in enough directions fast enough. In a breath, the field ahead of us disappeared and was replaced by a forest, and then another field behind that, and a small stream to the side, and then a river that the stream must flow into, and then – I think – through the haze of miles of empty air, mountains showed their silhouettes against the sky. But each second I looked there was more to see. I twisted my neck to both sides and struggled to see something that we'd just flown over as it slipped away behind, only to snap my gaze back to the front so I didn't miss what was coming.

I thought Miss E. was shouting behind me, and I struggled to hear, and then realized she was laughing and cheering. I twisted in my seat and could see her face behind the small windshield that was between us. She was smiling and had one hand raised in the air as if she were catching the air as it flowed past. I'd seen kids at school that were old enough to drive do the same in convertibles. They thought they were having the time of their lives. They had no idea what they were missing.

I couldn't resist raising my own arms above my head and letting out a cheer of my own. I wiggled in my seat as I flapped my imaginary wings in the air, and was surprised when my foot pushed into something on the floor. The plane reacted immediately. We turned to the left, but it was like the front half of the plane was still trying to pull us straight ahead while the tail was steering us someplace else. In one motion, my foot jumped off the pedal like it was on fire and I turned in my seat to look at Miss E. and make sure everything was OK. When I did, my knee caught the control stick, pushing it forward and to the side. Again, the plane's reaction was immediate.

The nose of the plane dropped down and the whine of the engine increased like we were picking up speed. At the same time we rolled to the left, and I was suddenly looking out the side of the plane at the ground below us. I scrambled for something on the opposite side to hold onto, forgetting the seat belt that was buckled firmly across my waist. Then as quickly as we had turned and tilted, we were straight and level again.

"Woohoo, that was exciting, huh? You having fun, Bets?" Miss E. called from behind with a laugh in her voice. Too nervous to take my hands off the edge of the cockpit, I only nodded. The view outside had changed. We'd come closer to the ground in the short second that the plane was tipping, and I wondered how many more seconds we would have had in the air if Miss E. hadn't straightened things out. I was suddenly very happy to have a world famous pilot at the controls behind me.

"All's well, Bets. We needed to start making some turns anyway. Nothing wrong with flying in a straight line when you have some place to go, but if that's all we're going to do we might as well be driving on a road. Go ahead, Bets. Take the stick."

I shook my head repeatedly, but Miss E.'s shouts of encouragement from behind finally convinced me. Gradually I slipped my right hand off the edge of the cockpit and curled my fingers around the control stick. I immediately felt the plane in my hand. There was resistance in the stick, and even though my knee had pushed it easily, I could feel that pushing it now would, in a way, be like pushing the whole plane.

Then my stick moved slightly to the left and I knew Miss E. was moving hers. The pedal under my right foot moved as well and bumped into my toe. I lifted both feet and rested them gently on the pedals, getting the same feeling of resistance that would move the plane if I wanted it to. We made a slow banked turn and it felt right this time, like the wings and tail and propeller were all working together. Then the stick came back to center and the pedals leveled out under my feet, and with them the plane came back to straight and level. We made the same gentle turn in the other direction, and I felt less like Miss E.'s movements were controlling mine and more like I was moving with her.

"Your turn, Bets!" I heard the shout from behind me. I hesitated, ready to shake my head no, but nodded instead. The stick moved more easily, and I guessed that Miss E. had removed her hand from it, though I hoped it was hovering near, ready to grab it in case I did something wrong. I mimicked the movements we'd just made, feeling more comfortable with the plane's shift and tilt because I knew it was coming and I was causing it.

"River!" I heard from the back seat, and when I had no reaction, she shouted again. "River!" My eyes caught the distant silver strip ahead to the left and I pointed the plane toward it. I felt Miss E. nudging the stick forward slightly and gradually bringing us closer to the ground. It was a whole different scene. Farm houses stood out in detail, and instead of forests or fields just being patches of green, I could now see individual trees or rows of crops. Then we were over the water and I was moving the stick slowly to one side and the other, following the gentle course of the river as it wound into the hills.

"Well that was just fine, Bets. Very well done." I could feel Miss E.'s hand again on the stick and took mine off to give her back full control. I didn't want to give up the feeling, didn't want the sense of being connected to the plane and the air around it to stop. But before I took my hand off, I promised myself plainly – I will do this again.

I was back to enjoying the scenery when the engine sound changed. Just a hiccup at first, quick enough to make me think I'd imagined it. Then it happened again, and again, until the engine was running noticeably rougher. The ground was closer and the duster now seemed less at home in the air. The rough engine coughed again, and then stopped. Except for the air whistling around us, we were suddenly plunged into silence. The blur of the propeller blades slowed until I could make out each individual blade, slowly turning in the wind like a child's pinwheel. The engine cranked once, and then again, before Miss E. shut it off entirely.

"No worries, Bets," a cheerful voice called from the rear cockpit. "Seatbelt buckled?" I gave a quick nod and turned around to see the same woman who had been sitting next to me in the Electra. Eyes smiling and hair tussled in the wind, Miss E. gave me a thumbs up. There was simply no way the woman behind me spent her days listening to quiet music in her armchair and sipping tomato juice in her kitchen. I saw in her at that moment the same energy and spirit that the crowds gathered at airfields to see forty years ago, and that my classmates walked by each day in their history classroom without noticing.

The ground was very close now. Trees that were just green patches minutes ago were now close enough to see individual branches that whipped by in a blur. Forest was on either side, and the river was still below us, but we were low enough that my view of the land ahead had been shortened to nothing. Then we were below the treetops, and the trees formed two thick green walls on either side of us. I could see the flaps on the wings moving constantly, and I was afraid to speak, knowing that Miss E. must be working the controls furiously. But I wanted to hear her voice and be reassured by it.

"No worries," she said again. I wasn't sure if she was talking to me or if she was telling herself, but it made me feel better nonetheless. The river we were following widened ahead then split, and when we reached that spot, Miss E. turned the plane to the left and took what looked like the smaller of the two branches. The trees were closer in, and branches struck one of the wing tips before Miss E centered the plane over the narrower strip of water.

Then the forest disappeared on our left side. The stream bent away to the right and took the trees with it. We found ourselves in the bright sun of a corn field just as the wheels slapped against the tall stalks. We sunk farther into the corn and then the wheels were bumping along the rutted ground while the wings plowed through the stalks and the still pin-wheeling propeller chewed them into dust. We hit a low spot that bumped us briefly into the air again, sailed over an open swath in the field that looked like a farm road, and came to a shuddering halt amongst the corn on the other side.

I kidded myself that it was sheer luck, that Miss E. had made a good guess with the left branch of the river, that we somehow ended up in the only flat patch of ground for miles. But I knew that if the woman sitting behind me was depending solely on luck, she would have used hers up long ago.

Dust hung in the afternoon sun, the air suddenly silent and still. I heard Miss E. pull herself from the cockpit and then saw her climb over onto the wing and hop nimbly to the ground. She looked up at me with a smile on her face and her hands on her hips.

"Well, come on, Bets. Not the place I had in mind for our picnic, but it seems like it will do."

Lessons

The air above the corn field was still and hot. Dust hung as if captured in a photograph. Only the buzzing bees seemed capable of moving in the suspended air. The rows of corn stretched out around us in all directions, but we pushed through it until we reached the road. The tail of the duster still stuck out beyond the last row of corn, and Miss E. sat down at the edge of the road in its shadow and gestured for me to join her, like crash landing a crop duster in a corn field and then sitting down to a relaxing lunch was the most natural thing in the world.

From the patch of shade, our flight seemed a distant memory. The duster sat as if it had always been in the field, and Miss E. spread a picnic blanket out on the dirt road. Even though it wasn't the place she said she had in mind, it felt like the exact right place, and it didn't seem possible that we'd reached the spot in a powerless plane that was very quickly falling out of the air. But I still felt like Miss E. had some explaining to do.

"What happened up there?"

She smiled pleasantly and responded in a voice that sounded like we'd done nothing all morning but lounge in a corn field. "Up where? Oh, the plane do you mean?"

"Of course I mean the plane? What happened? The engine stopped."

"Exactly, Bets. It would seem you've asked and answered your question in the same breath. Well done, although I suppose you could have saved yourself the talking and me the listening. Have a deviled egg, Bets." She smiled again and winked before putting half a deviled egg in her mouth and then rolling her eyes in pleasure.

She was different. I'd seen Miss E. in a way that none of the other people in town had. When she went to town, she was playing the part of the grouchy old lady who never talked to anyone and only grumbled under her breath. She let that guise fade away for me, but when I saw her in the cornfield I realized the Miss E. I'd gotten to know while sitting at her kitchen table wasn't entirely the real Miss E. either. Not really, at least not the way she used to be. The kitchen table Miss E. was resigned to living out her life stuck on a farm with a plane hidden away in a barn, resigned to living with thirty year old choices gone sour, resigned to not really living at all. But the Miss E. I met in the corn field was full of life. She smiled, she giggled, and seemed to want nothing more than to be exactly where she was at that moment doing exactly what she was doing. I realized that this was how Miss E. used to be, back when she was flying, back when she could be Amelia Earhart for real.

"Pickle?" She bit in with a crunch and another eye roll.

"But the engine stopped. Why did the engine stop?"

"Oh, Bets. Get over it. Back when I started flying, if you had a flight without the engine dying or the flaps practically falling off the wings, it was a good one. We had good luck on this one. We were high enough to have a good long glide, and this field was as good a landing spot as any. We could have been swimming. Fruit salad?"

Miss E. continued to pull out a limitless variety of food from the basket. How she had fit it all into the small space was a mystery, and I began to wonder if the extra weight of the picnic was to blame for our untimely and unplanned landing.

"So, tell me about your mother." The sudden shift in conversation erased all thought of airplane engines and picnic baskets from my mind. I stumbled through a few words about her playing bridge with the neighbors and some of her favorite meals to cook before a look from Miss E. told me that this was not what she was asking about. "Come on, Bets. People spend so much time wondering about me when I come to town, they don't realize how much listening and watching can be done when a body's not talking all the time. There's no limit to the gossip I overhear when I'm out and about or the things I happen to notice that no one else does because they're all too busy looking at me. And even if I didn't, I'd have to wonder why a girl whose father's been away for months is sitting around with me instead of keeping her mother company and helping around the house. Between school, grocery deliveries, research in the library, and taking up space at my kitchen table, you're spending a considerable amount of time avoiding home. So, fess up, Bets."

I started to say something but then didn't because I didn't really know what to say. I sighed. I shrugged my shoulders. I threw up my hands and rolled my eyes as if to say there was nothing to talk about, but I didn't actually say it because I knew there was something to talk about. I looked down at the blanket in front of me and pulled off little pieces of lint, hoping Miss E. would eventually give up and say something so I didn't have to. But she simply sat in front of me, occasionally taking a bite of food off her plate. I checked occasionally by trying to lift my eyes as far as they would go without raising my head.

I finally let loose with a frustrated growl and a string of run on sentences. "What do you want me to say? Do you want to hear about how emotionless my mother is? How there are no good days or bad days with her, just bridge games and crock pot suppers and look how white the laundry came out this week. I could talk about the same three or four questions she asks me at the dinner table every night to make it seem like we're actually having a normal conversation, but even worse than that is the time when she doesn't talk, not really talk anyway. Like a trip to the grocery store, not Johnson's but all the way into Santa Rosa, the whole drive without a word and then nothing but get a can of this or a box of that and then nothing the whole ride home until I'm ready to explode because I can't possibly believe that someone could go that long without talking. No talking at all, like she's not interested in what I have to say or what's going on in my life or even just to tell me something interesting that happened to her. But that's the easy stuff, that's the stuff I'm sure every kid deals with, the parents that don't know how to talk to them. I'm lucky I just have one, right? But the part that really has me walking around the house like there's a piano hanging over my head ready to fall, is talking about my father. Because that never happens, but every second that I'm home I think that it must be about to happen. Surely today she'll say something. Maybe after dinner. Maybe before bed. Maybe in an hour, or a minute, or in a second, or two. But she never, never does. She reads his letters, but that's not talking. Not a sit down, 'Hey how are you doing? Yes, I miss him too.' I miss my dad. I miss him, and I'm afraid of what could happen to him, and there's one other person in the world who should miss him and worry about him as much as me, but she doesn't say anything. Ever."

Then I cried. A good old pull my knees to my chin, bury my face in my hands cry. I figured any second Miss E. would put her hand on my shoulder, and I was ready to shrug it off. It didn't come and I was relieved, but at the same time I was hurt that she wasn't coming over to comfort me. I'm ashamed to admit it, but I dragged out my cry for an extra minute or so giving her time to put her arm around me or say, "There, there, it will be OK." But she didn't. When I lifted my head and wiped the tears off my cheeks with the palms of my hands, I was surprised to see Miss E. still picking at the remains of our picnic, gazing at the sky, and looking like her thoughts were far away.

I was about to say something when she sprung to her feet faster than I would have thought she could. "Well, I suppose I should take a look at that engine and figure out if we'll be flying home or hitchhiking. Judging from the traffic that's been by, it could be a long walk." She ducked under a wing and disappeared toward the front of the plane, leaving me red eyed and wet cheeked and feeling like I'd just poured my heart out to the corn stalks surrounding me.

Fresh tears came at the feeling of betrayal I had from being pushed into talking and then promptly ignored, but I choked them back and stormed off after Miss E. I found her standing on a small step built into the side of the plane with the engine cover open. She was peering in and didn't look up when I approached.

"I can't believe you listened to me say all that and then..." I spouted before I was cut off.

"Ah, Bets. Glad you came up here. Be a dear and dig under my seat for a tool box. I'm pretty sure Fred keeps one there in case of emergency. Not that our little adventure constitutes one, but having a few tools on hand would certainly make this little fix-up job go faster."

I bit my tongue, grumbling the rest of what I wanted to say, and climbed up on the wing to search for the tool box.

"Fuel pump stopped," Miss E. said when I returned with the small metal box. I couldn't imagine there was anything in it that could fix an airplane, but I handed the box up to her anyway. I crossed my arms waiting for some response from Miss E., and when none came I turned away ready to stomp off down the farm road in whatever direction would take me toward home. But a call of "I could use a hand up here," from Miss E. stopped me in my tracks.

I struggled to get my foot up to the small step on the side of the duster, and wondered how the seventy-year-old woman above me had done it. She reached down to pull me up, but I hesitated to take her hand thinking I might pull her down on top of me. Miss E. sighed and grabbed my wrist, giving me enough lift to reach the step and clamber up to the engine. "Come on, Bets. We're not climbing Mt. Everest here."

The greasy parts of the engine I saw sticking out from the duster before we took off were a pretty good indication of what was under the engine cover. Any parts not covered in grease were coated with a thick layer of rust. I secretly crossed my fingers with the hope that Miss E. wouldn't be able to get it started again and decided that the long walk down the farm road would be the best option.

Balancing on the small step next to Miss E., I could understand why she needed some help. The curve of the plane made it difficult to stand on the step without holding on with one hand. So she was forced to work with one hand, grabbing tools and reaching down into the engine while she held onto the edge of the engine compartment with the other. When she'd said she needed a hand, she meant it. With me handing her tools and taking engine parts from her, the job was much easier.

She talked while she worked and told me what she was doing and what she thought the problem was. Since the engine had just stopped running without any signs of smoke or unusual noises, Miss E. suspected the fuel pump. It would be an easy fix she thought, but getting to it meant taking off several parts. She told me what each part was as she handed it to me and explained what it did. I set each carefully in the cradle formed where the engine cover met the windshield, and hoped I'd be able to remember which was which when she asked for them again. The fuel pump finally reached, Miss E. discovered a broken wire and was able to strip the rubber insulation off back to a stronger section of wire and reconnect it to the pump.

Reassembly of the engine went quickly, and I was ready to hop off the step to the ground below when Miss E. put her hand on top of mine and held it there against the edge of the engine compartment. She looked me in the eye with a stare that made me want to turn away to the ground or the sky or anywhere else, but I couldn't.

"I'm not one to tell folks what to do, Bets. I always went my own way and followed my own ideas. I don't want anyone telling me what to do now, didn't want it when I was your age. So I won't tell you how to act or think toward your mother. And I never had kids of my own, so I can't say much about parenting, but I think I have a pretty good idea of where your mother is coming from.

"I wasn't much older than you when World War I hit, and I saw my fair share of kids' fathers go away and not come back. Then I lost Sam in World War II. After that, they stopped numbering the wars, so I suppose that means they're getting smaller, but it doesn't seem like that's so and they sure do seem to involve the whole world even if they don't call 'em that."

She looked up at the sky, tracing the path of a cloud, and paused long enough that I thought she was done talking, then her eyes returned to mine. "My point is that I think your mother and I might see eye to eye when it comes to dealing with a war and someone you love." With that, she hopped down. I turned to follow, but she was standing right where I would land so I was forced to stay on the step and look down at her while she looked back up at me with her hands on her hips.

"Might be your mom's way of dealing with your father being away is to get quiet about it and keep things inside. And that might not fit with what you need from her or how you expect her to be, but that's just too bad for you." Miss E. stood below me for another moment waiting to see if I had a response, then she turned and climbed up on the wing. "Close and latch that engine cover before you hop down, OK Bets?"

I stood balanced on the step with her last thought stuck in my head. I'd expected Miss E to take my side. After all, I was the one with the mother that wouldn't acknowledge that my father was away fighting a war. But my tearful outpouring on the picnic blanket seemed liked it had happened to someone else. According to Miss E., I was the problem and it was my mother who had all the troubles. I turned all this over in my head as I struggled to close the engine compartment without slamming my fingers in it. Finally closed and latched, I jumped down to the ground, feeling more confused than I had before I'd stepped up.

Our exit from the corn field was almost as exciting as our entry. Miss E. called me back toward the tail, and together we lifted it off the ground. I suppose an airplane needs to be light in order fly through the air, but because I knew I'd be climbing into it and trusting my life to it, I wanted it to be heavier, more substantial. With its tail no longer dragging, and its big wheels rolling easily along the furrows, Miss E. and I had enough pull to get the duster fully out onto the farm road and pointing down its length.

Fuel pump fixed, at least for the moment, the engine roared to life, and we careened down the road, the lower wings of the duster chopping off corn stalks as we went. I gripped the edge of the cockpit again, waiting for the bump of the wheels on the dirt road to turn into the smooth glide of wings in the air, and thought about what Miss E had said. Did I really have any expectations for my mother? She had always been the way she was, I thought. She had always been flat, emotionless, she'd always just moved on with the business of the day to day without reaction. It had been my father who reacted. A big grin, a laugh, or a tearful eye and a hug when I needed it. I realized as the duster cleared the corn field and soared once again into the sky that what I was really looking for wasn't a change in my mother, what I really needed and wanted was to have my father home again.

The stick between my knees pushed forward under Miss E.'s control and the plane stopped its climb and leveled off. I watched the throttle knob push in slightly and the roar of the engine quieted to a steady hum. I felt almost sleepy as the afternoon sun and the vibrations lulled me. So much so that I jumped a little when Miss E.'s voice shouted over the noise of the plane and the air rushing past.

"One thing you've got to remember, Bets, is that your mother is missing your father even more than you are, even if she doesn't show it. A daughter and a father, well, that's something special, but you don't know what it's like to be a wife yet... to love a husband."

Miss E. had all the time she needed to continue talking to me in a quiet corn field, but she'd clammed up and set to work getting the plane in the air again like our conversation was done. Then once we were back in the sky, sitting one behind the other with engine noise filling the air as it rushed past us, she started up chatting again. But like everything she did, there was reason behind it. There was time to think as we got the duster pointed in the right direction, as the horizon slipped below us, and the landscape spread out around us. Maybe she needed time to think about what to say next, but more likely she knew I needed time to consider what she'd told me while fixing the engine. She'd waited until I'd realized something, and then she gave me a little bit more to think about.

My reply was on my lips. My defense, my reasons for why I knew that I loved my father more than my mother did. But the throttle knob moved again, and the engine noise increased in pitch and volume. Miss E. had let me know this was a one way conversation – her talking, me thinking.

Our landing at the airstrip was uneventful. As we walked back to the red pickup, Fred Noonan's figure was silhouetted in the opening of a hanger. Miss E. raised a hand, and he waved back in reply. There was no mention of the problem with the fuel pump or our emergency cornfield landing. I expected the drive home to bring another installment in our conversation about my mother, but Miss E. only asked a few questions about school and told little stories about some of the places we drove by. She had clearly said all there was to say on the topic. As far as changing my perspective, the rest was up to me.

Twenty Words

If Miss E. meant for the flight in the duster to change me in some way, it didn't work. Like going back to school after discovering that Miss E was really Amelia Earhart, I expected a change. I thought things would somehow be noticeably different, but the days after our flight were like any others.

Life with my mother was unchanged, and that was the whole point of Miss E. taking me flying. A different perspective, she'd said. Well, other than half scaring the pants off of me, the flight hadn't done anything to change my feelings toward my mother, and Miss E.'s little pep talk with me in the cornfield hadn't made me any more understanding toward my mother's lack of emotion.

I gave it an honest try. I brought up my father a couple times at the dinner table, when I normally would have remained silent. My mother seemed a little surprised, but she dodged the topic as skillfully as ever. I asked a couple questions after she'd read a letter from him one night, hoping to start a conversation, but she only smiled and sighed and folded up the letter. After a week of trying, I let myself slip back into my old routine of keeping to myself and nodding politely when my mother talked about the weather or the neighbors.

School wasn't any different either, other than my feeling like telling everyone I saw in the hallways that I'd gone flying with Amelia Earhart. Heck, I would have been happy just to tell Anne or Cassie or Susan that I'd gone flying at all. As far as weekend activities went, I figured I could top anyone's story about softball wins, first dates, or even first kisses. But of course, I couldn't tell anyone anything.

Our tally in Mr. Flynn's class was inching higher. I hadn't given away Amelia Earhart's identity yet, but it was looking like I would need to soon if we were going to win the trip to San Francisco. We'd been using what I'd discovered in the library that day – what the class had come to call "Flynn's Rules" even though we'd never talked to Mr. Flynn about them.

1. Look for connections with other famous Americans. This category was ripe with results. We'd found four First Ladies who were definitely more deserving of a place on Mr. Flynn's wall than their husbands were.
2. Come up with a list of likely suspects. We came up with a list of our top one hundred Americans, and then went through the list crossing names off once we'd double checked their photos and compared it to what we could find in the library. Mr. Flynn had slipped in five that had made our list as well, but we'd missed them on our first run through the library because of rule number three.

3. Look beyond the iconic photos. Theodore Roosevelt before the pince-nez and mustache, Marilyn Monroe while she was still Norma Jean. Yep, those and others had been staring down at us from Mr. Flynn's walls all year.

We were down to three. I knew I'd be giving up Amelia Earhart soon. I wouldn't be telling anyone about Miss E. of course. Even though it felt like the only thing happening in the world, other than Mr. Flynn's students, most people in Forestville had no idea about the pictures on our classroom wall and if they did, they didn't care. So there wasn't much chance that me revealing the identity of the smiling messy haired woman on the wall would cause someone in town to guess that the little old lady who lived five miles outside of town was Amelia Earhart. But I was still nervous about it.

I had to get her twenty words right. It didn't matter that no one outside my class would even know what I wrote and most of them wouldn't even bother to read it, they'd be so distracted by winning the trip. I'd know what I wrote, and unlike all the other photos in the classroom, I knew the woman I'd be writing about. I'd sat at her kitchen table. I'd sat in her airplane. I had to get her words right.

I started working on it when we had five pictures left, mulling ideas over in my mind when I should have been paying attention in class. Mr. Flynn caught me once, scribbling phrases in the margins of my notebook. He didn't say anything, just raised an eyebrow and walked up the aisle.

"Something bothering you, Bets?" Miss E. asked one afternoon while we sat at her table. I hesitated, not really knowing if something was bothering me, not really sure where my thoughts had been. She'd thankfully not brought up my mother since our flight weeks ago. But I realized while figuring out what to say in response to her question, that I had been thinking about the words I'd need to write. I'd been so focused, I was scowling.

I told her. I knew trying to hide the truth wasn't an option with Miss E. Part of me hoped that she might offer to help, might even insist on helping to make sure I got it right. That part of me was wrong. Miss E. just nodded and was silent. A long silence, but I knew her well enough now to know the conversation wasn't over. I wondered if she knew that I knew. That I knew about the trick she played with those long silences, and I wondered if she was making them longer on purpose, giving me more time to think, or doing it simply to annoy me because I was on to her.

"Well, Bets," she said at last, "You'll get it right. Come show me when you do."

I had long ago figured out that Miss E.'s way of helping someone was to give them absolutely no help at all, so it didn't surprise me that she didn't offer to sit down with me that afternoon and co-write her twenty words. What caught me off guard was the notion that Miss E. would be seeing what I wrote about her. I knew I had to get those words right. For myself I wanted them right. For my classmates who would be reading them, and for Mr. Flynn. It never occurred to me that I would be writing them for Miss E.'s eyes. I left her kitchen feeling worse than when I'd entered, but there was no taking it back. Miss E. knew about the assignment now; she'd be expecting to see the words I wrote about her.

Woody Guthrie fell prey a few days later, and Marian Anderson bit the dust right after him. Amelia was one of only two photographs left. When Sammy Wilks turned in his twenty words on George Washington Carver, I was determined not to leave school until I finished writing mine. I asked Mr. Flynn if I could come to his room after school.

I'd never really stayed after school before other than going to the library. But that didn't count. There were the kids who stayed for sports or play practice and the student council kids who always seemed to be decorating the gym for a dance. There were the kids who'd gotten in trouble or hadn't turned in an assignment and the kids who were struggling and stayed after for extra help from a teacher. I didn't fit into any of those groups, which was probably why Mr. Flynn's eyebrows shot up when I asked him, the same way he'd done when he caught me editing Amelia's words during class. But he agreed to see me at the end of the day.

He was working when I came in, grading papers probably. If Mr. Flynn was curious at all about why I wanted to work in his classroom after school, he didn't show it. He lifted his head when I came in and gave me a smile, but then quickly went back to work with whatever was on his desk.

When I'd asked him if I could stay, I didn't really know why I thought it would be easier to work in Mr. Flynn's room, it just seemed right. But once I'd lifted my head to take a short break from writing, I'd realized I'd made the right choice. There in front of me was Amelia, curly-haired and smiling. I couldn't have asked for better inspiration.

I don't know how long I worked. It was long enough that Mr. Flynn had finished whatever work he'd had on his desk, but he was respectful enough of my need that he busied himself with other things. I only caught him checking the clock once. I let my thoughts wander enough to wonder what Mr. Flynn's life was like outside of his classroom. He didn't wear a ring, so I knew there wasn't a wife waiting for him at home. But a girlfriend? This had been lunch time conversation more than once. Most of the girls had decided that Mr. Flynn was handsome enough and that there must be a girlfriend. The only question was whether they talked about anything other than U.S. history when they went out on dates.

But that could be left to lunchtime. I had work to do. As I scribbled and crossed out, I kept thinking about the Quick Facts section of the elementary school Amelia Earhart book I'd found in the library, and how that author had chosen the word "disappear". Maybe it was just the word that made the most sense, but it seemed to me a careful choice, like it was a word that said what had happened but at the same time left the reader wondering what really happened. It was a word that just took up space on the page, one that your eye could skim over so you could move along to the next one, except that it nagged a little, causing you to jump back, reread, and think about what was really meant. Those were the sort of words I was looking for.

I had a lot to say in those twenty words. Finishing up Mr. Flynn's challenge and getting to San Francisco was starting to feel secondary to what I really needed to accomplish. I had to recognize all that Amelia had done, and how influential she was. But if that's all I did, my twenty words would have been no better than the quick facts section in the Earhart book for kids.

I knew the rest of her story, or at least the rest of the story so far. Who else knew that? I couldn't resist weaving that in, finding a way to not tell the secret, but tell it at the same time.

And then there was the Electra, sitting in that barn touched only by stray sunbeams filtering through hay dust. Miss E. had to fly that plane again, had to finish what she'd started. I think maybe the idea entered my mind the day I'd talked to Miss E. about the twenty words and she'd told me to show them to her when I'd finished. Maybe I didn't realize it, or maybe I didn't want to admit it, but what I hoped, what I really hoped, was that I could write something that would convince Miss E. to fly again.

But twenty was not a lot of words.

I stared at the paper that was currently on my desk, the only one that hadn't been crumpled and discarded. There were about twenty words on it, but they did nothing but complete Mr. Flynn's assignment. In frustration, I tore the paper in half and brushed the halves off my desk in different directions. The left half somersaulted to the floor and landed face up where it could taunt me with its half sentences. I bent to grab it and crumple it into a ball too, but I stopped before I did and read what was there.

And what was there reminded me of some of the poems we'd read in English class the month before. Short little poems with no rhymes that had kids immediately raising their hands to debate whether they were really poems at all. They said a lot with just a few words on each line, with thoughts that seemed to carry over from one line to the next. Sometimes an idea got broken up between lines, where you'd think the writing was saying one thing but then you'd finish the next line and realize the writer really meant something else. And sometimes you'd have to read the poem over and over again before you realized what it was saying. That was exactly what I needed to do.

I looked at my half sheet of paper and pulled a fresh one from my binder. And then I started writing again, taking my words from the torn sheet and using them again, but breaking up the sentences, no longer striving for the perfect paragraph, instead thinking in lines; not worrying if a thought got broken up between two lines, instead trying to do it on purpose. After some furious scribbling, crossing out, and more scribbling, I finally put my pen down with a definitive smack on my desk and read what I had.

Amelia Earhart

When
Amelia Earhart circled the world,
she captivated us.
She lives
in her accomplishments.
I found her
an inspiration.
Fly!

It wasn't going to win any poetry awards, but I wasn't trying for an award.

I didn't say anything. I just walked my paper up to the front of the room and put it on Mr. Flynn's now empty desk. He only read the name at the top of the page before he started nodding, and his eyes flicked up to mine to let me know I had the right person, something I'd known for months. But when he continued reading, his expression changed. I could see his eyes move up the page to reread the lines again. He let out a quiet "huh," which was part question, but mostly statement. He lifted his eyes up again to make contact with mine and I felt like he was scanning my face, looking for an expression that would give away what my words were hiding. When he didn't find it, he put my paper down on his desk and his hand went to his chin to scratch his thin beard as his eyes tracked back and forth reading what I'd written one more time.

"This is some interesting writing, Elizabeth." He paused and I had no idea what was coming next. "I have ninety-nine other papers from your classmates about the people on the walls. Some of them clearly struggling to keep under the twenty word limit, others I think, happy that's all they had to write. But all of them are as factual and boring as an encyclopedia. Your writing really says a lot, and it says it in a way that makes the reader think. Nicely done. Congratulations Elizabeth, it looks like your class is going to San Francisco."

Fire

I had never been on a school bus. All of the base schools I attended were close enough to walk to, and El Molino was just a short bike ride away. Between needing my bike for after school deliveries and simply wanting to ride it every chance I got, there hadn't been a day that I'd stooped to riding on the noisy yellow school bus.

I imagine a high school bus is a jungle on a good day, fill it with excited teenagers headed for San Francisco and you've got a riot on your hands. I sat near the front of the bus with a couple girls I'd gotten to know from working on Mr. Flynn's class project. We had a pretty good view of the scenery ahead and could avoid most of the chaos happening in the back seats. We were also just a seat behind Mr. Flynn and could chat with him during the ride. He was a teacher, but he was also pretty cool.

Several times he stood up and raised his peace sign toward the roof of the bus. This was mildly effective but it wasn't long before the volume ramped up again. Finally, he stood and rather than flashing the peace sign, he pointed. He had an expression on his face that we rarely saw in his classroom and the response was immediate silence. I don't know how the student that walked toward the front of the bus knew that Mr. Flynn was pointing at him, but he arrived a few seconds later and plunked himself into the seat next to Mr. Flynn. After that, the bus ride was relatively calm and we had a chance to talk about what, and more importantly who, we hoped to see in the city.

A group of us had gotten together the weekend before the trip to listen to records in someone's basement, and one of the songs played was a new record by a singer named Scott McKenzie. We'd never heard of him before, but the song was on all the radio stations, and because of its title and lyrics it was a perfect anthem for our trip. Once the bus had quieted, you could hear a number of students humming the melody of "San Francisco," and like the song suggested many of the girls had put flowers in their hair. We didn't know what Scott McKenzie looked like, but if he happened to be hanging out on the streets of San Francisco with Janis, Grace, or Jerry, we'd be happy to meet him.

As the bus pulled off the highway and wound its way through the city streets, our faces pressed the windows. It didn't take long for a bunch of kids from a small town to forget who we were looking for, as we craned our necks to see the buildings that towered above. We were all excited, and the bus was filled with chatter whether we saw our idols on the street corners or not. Before we knew it, the bus was pulling to the side of the street and we filed off into a plaza in front of City Hall.

The voice on the megaphone was the first thing I noticed. Maybe hearing the drone of the school bus for hours made my ears overly sensitive, but the voice was grating and seemed aggressive even though the words were lost to distortion.

As we walked across the plaza, my eyes scanned the scene and found the source of the voice. A man stood about halfway up the steps to the building. He faced out toward the plaza and seemed to be preaching to the pedestrians hurrying off to their offices, but occasionally he turned to point the megaphone at City Hall as if addressing a particular comment to those inside.

His voice was still garbled, and I could only make out a few words at a time. "Police action... illegal... Vietnam." The last one made me stop in my tracks and turn to look, but whoever was behind me in line walked right into me and grumbled an irritated, "Hey, com' on."

I started walking again, and as we got closer to City Hall I got a better look at the man behind the megaphone. I had never seen a hippie, but I knew what they were I guess. Most adults would call the musicians we were hoping to spot in San Francisco hippies, and more than a few of them would label us with the term just for listening to their music. I didn't think Janis and Jerry were hippies, and I didn't think of myself as one, but I was pretty sure the man with the megaphone fit the bill.

He wore clothes that looked like they were hand-me-downs of hand-me-downs. His pants, covered in patches, drooped on his skinny waist. Over his tie-dyed shirt was an old army jacket. Where the insignias had been were gaping holes, as if tearing the patches off wasn't enough and the fabric beneath had to be ripped away as well. There was anger and desperation in his voice, like he couldn't help but shout his message, and the arm not holding the megaphone gestured violently to emphasize his point.

Mr. Johnson grumbled about hippies from behind his newspaper most afternoons. He sometimes called them "freaks," or when there was a particularly offensive piece of news, "pinko commies." I got the sense that Mr. Johnson was more troubled by their political views than their musical tastes though, so Janis and Jerry were probably safe. But if the man shouting from the city hall steps was a hippie (or a pinko commie for that matter), I knew I didn't want to be one.

"Stop American imperialism!" his voice squawked through the megaphone. "Stop this illegal war!" As we walked past, the amplified voice was loud enough to hurt. I scowled and covered my ears. The man must have taken my reaction as disagreement and directed his next pronouncement at me. "American soldiers have the blood of children on their hands!" His eyes glared at me over the top of the megaphone and followed me until I turned away and broke into a run, pushing my way to the head of the line past Mr. Flynn, not stopping until I'd reached the top of the steps and put a stone pillar between us.

Now I understood Mr. Johnson's anger at the headlines he read. That hippie was wrong, and I wished I had a megaphone of my own so I could tell him so. How could he know what he was talking about anyway? My father was over there, so I knew. American soldiers were in Vietnam helping people. They were protecting them from communism. That must be a good thing. If it wasn't, my father wouldn't be over there doing it.

A soft touch on my shoulder made me realize that I was squeezing my eyes shut and digging my fingernails into my palms. Mr. Flynn was standing over me.

"Everything OK, Elizabeth?" he said in a voice that told me he knew everything certainly was not.

"Yeah... Sure... Just a lot of steps to climb." I said, adding a couple deep breaths for effect.

A quick glance down the steps toward the hippie was enough to show me that Mr. Flynn had already figured me out. "Lots of opinions in a big city, Elizabeth. We can cover our ears when we hear one we don't like, or we can choose to listen to all of them and try to figure things out for ourselves," he said in a voice that was different than the one he used in his classroom, not like he was teaching me something but like he was sharing something that he knew. "And besides," Mr. Flynn continued as he opened the door for me, "You ride your bike all over town every afternoon. You could climb those stairs ten times without breaking a sweat."

The tour of City Hall was what you'd expect from a field trip to an office building. We saw some rooms with desks and typewriters that all looked the same, but as we entered each one Mr. Flynn's friend explained how it served a unique and important role in the functioning of the city. That may be true, but I'm not sure because none of us listened.

The highlight of the tour, which isn't saying much, came when we all filed into the press briefing room. The room didn't look anything like the fifteen other rooms we had been in, so that was a positive. Normally, the space would be filled with reporters waiting to get the scoop on some announcement from the mayor, but either they'd cleared the room to make way for our class, or more likely it was just a slow news day. We sat in the chairs that would normally be filled with reporters and listened when Mr. Flynn's friend stood at the podium in the front of the room and explained why a press briefing room had a unique and important role in the functioning of the city. He went on to tell us that he had hoped the mayor would be able to meet with us but there was an important development and he couldn't make it. Instead we were each given an official City of San Francisco pen and a pad of paper with the city's emblem printed on it. Mr. Flynn, whose enthusiasm for our trip to City Hall had been limitless and totally unrelated to the music scene, seemed unfazed at the way things had turned out. We collected our things and gave a chorus of thank you's to Mr. Flynn's friend, then we wound our way back though several of the unique and important rooms and ended up back in the lobby.

I knew something was different before we even made it through the doors. I could hear it. There was still a garbled voice on the megaphone, but behind it there was something else. Something that sounded like the ocean. I half expected to see waves crashing against the steps when we exited the building. And in a way, I did.

There were people. Hundreds? A thousand? Too many to count. The plaza between the steps and the street had disappeared and in its place was a sea of bodies, some with arms raised and peace signs flashing, but many more had curled their two-fingered peace sign into a shaking fist. They were mostly hippies like the man with the megaphone, lots of them. But there were other people too. People that looked like they could be working behind a restaurant counter or selling newspapers at a stand on the corner if they weren't outside City Hall shouting.

"No war! No war! No war!" It was easier to understand once we were outside the doors. A constant pulse of voices. Waves crashing. It sounded like the ocean, but it looked like a fire. We were right in front of the center where things seemed the hottest, where everyone had an angry face and a fist in the air. And that anger seemed to be spreading, catching the ones who were next to it, and the ones next to them. Farther out on the edges things were just starting to warm up, but those people kept pressing closer, moving toward the heat in the center and catching its flame. And beyond that were the sparks, people just walking by on the street or strolling through a nearby park. Just regular people until they heard the noise or saw the crowd and came closer, closer still, and then caught fire too.

There was no going down the steps. Pick your metaphor. We'd be diving into the ocean, walking into the flames. Either way it wasn't happening. Mr. Flynn's calm was shaken. His head turned side to side, taking in the crowd, and then back toward the doors like he wasn't quite sure which way we should go. Mr. Flynn's friend must have figured out something was wrong and followed us through the doors. He stood beside him and over the chanting I could hear bits of their shouted conversation.

"...wanted them to see..."

"...ever this big?"

"... never like this before."

It was easy to fill in the missing bits. Just like us, Mr. Flynn had an agenda of his own for our trip. He wasn't interested in the music scene, but he wasn't interested in the insider's tour of City Hall either. And if we'd thought at all about what Mr. Flynn had told us about the trip rather than getting so worked up over who we might see on a street corner, we'd have realized that the trip to City Hall wasn't Mr. Flynn's style at all. He taught us to be thinkers, to exercise our curiosity, and to question the way things were. There was no way he'd have made such a big deal about touring an office building. Maybe if we were going to sit down with the mayor for a question and answer session, but Mr. Flynn would have made us prepare for that, would have had us writing questions weeks in advance and tossing out the ones that didn't address an important issue.

No, Mr. Flynn didn't bring us to San Francisco to see what was inside City Hall. He wanted us to see what was happening outside. He wanted a bunch of kids from Small-town, USA, to see what some people thought about what was going on in Vietnam, wanted us to discover that there was more to current events than Mr. Johnson's newspaper headlines. But the mob scene that was steadily growing on the steps below us was more than he'd bargained for. We were no longer witnessing current events. We were about to become part of one.

Before Mr. Flynn and his friend had a chance to figure out how to get twenty-five teenagers through a crowd of hippies, freaks, and pinko commies, the situation went from bad to worse. The wail of a siren could be heard over the roar of the crowd and three or four police cars appeared. The reaction was immediate, as if someone tossed a can of gasoline into the fire.

The crowd exploded. For those on the fringes, the arrival of the police meant that the party was over and they needed to disappear as quickly as possible. They'd been on their way to someplace else anyway and had only gotten distracted by the shouting. Hurry along to your job in the restaurant or selling papers on the corner. But for the angriest, the ones in the hottest part of the fire, the police were just another part of what they were protesting – the government, the army, the police—just different parts of the same broken machine. A moment ago the crowd was protesting soldiers in far away Vietnam, but uniforms were uniforms and their ire immediately turned on the blue ones emerging from the police cars. For one breathless second, I thought that the crowd was about to attack the police. It didn't seem possible for that much anger to stay in one place. But instead, they moved away from the police and toward the doors of City Hall.

I didn't have time to think about it then. Replaying the scene in my mind later, I tried to puzzle out why things happened the way they did. Maybe some protesters were just trying to get away from the police, and through the doors was the only way to go. Maybe some knew they were minutes away from getting hauled down to the police station and figured they might as well make the most of the time they had to get their point across. The most calculating must have known that the police were the tipping point, creating enough anger that the crowd could be nudged to do anything. Whatever the reason, the protesters in front of us collectively decided that they all needed to get into City Hall.

In a blink I lost my vantage point at the top of the steps and became a part of the scene I had been watching. Faces flashed by me. I stumbled but didn't fall, bodies pressed so tightly together that I couldn't fall. I would catch a glimpse of a classmate, and then they would be gone.

The surge squeezed the breath from my lungs. People pushing, people being pushed from behind, and more behind them, all rushing toward City Hall. But the doors opened out, and we were getting crushed against them. I tried to scream, but there was no room for it. And then somehow, mercifully, someone got a door open and the crowd spilled through like a flood.

All I wanted to do was get away, to move far from the chaos at the doors, but instead I was pushed toward it. Another door was opened, then another, and the flow through them increased. I moved without taking steps. If I'd stayed where I was, the crowd would have washed over me, so instead I moved with it as it surged through the doors.

The spacious lobby made running instantly possible. People ran toward the stairway, people ran toward the elevators. I set my sights on what seemed to be a protected alcove with a few chairs and a telephone booth. I was hit to one side or the other a few times and spun around once as people rushed passed, but I finally made it to the wall next to the telephone, with a chair between me and the flow of protesters.

I took what felt like my first breath in hours. I wanted to close my eyes. I wanted to put my arms in front of my face and bring my knees to my chin, but instead I scanned the room for a familiar face. I found one behind the information desk in the center of the lobby. Like me, Mr. Flynn had found a safe place to get out of the endless flow of bodies moving through the lobby. A familiar face, but he no longer looked like my teacher. In class he was in charge, and something as small as a raised peace sign was enough to bring things to order. But the Mr. Flynn behind the information desk looked utterly helpless. He was responsible for an entire class of high school students, and he had lost every last one of them. His head jerked from side to side and his eyes flashed around the room trying to take in every face that passed him, but seeing none of them. And there was something more. There was disappointment. He wanted us to see a protest, wanted us to see Americans exercising their right to be heard. But what we were in now wasn't being heard, wasn't exercising a right. It was creating chaos, and whether Mr. Flynn believed in their cause or not, he didn't approve of what was unfolding around him.

For one crazy second, I thought about crossing the lobby and going to Mr. Flynn. Going to him and telling him that it was OK, that I got it, that I understood that people were upset, that they could disagree, and that they needed a voice. And then she hit me. Or more accurately, she was hit into me.

The police had arrived. I don't know if the police from outside had finally made it up the steps and through the doors or if they had come from inside the building, but suddenly they were everywhere. Until that day, in my mind policemen hid behind billboards waiting for speeders. They wrote parking tickets, and they drove their cars with lights flashing in the Labor Day parade. These police raised clubs and hit anyone within swinging distance. They pushed them into walls and twisted their arms until they fell to the floor. Then they moved on to the next one.

There was a shift. People stopped running up the stairway, and they'd stopped pushing through the doors. Now they were moving in reverse, trying to get out, trying to get away. But it didn't matter. The police still came, still hit and pushed.

I saw her running. Her long sandy blond hair was flowing out behind her like the flowery dress she wore. She was darting in one direction and then another, desperately trying to get away and not knowing which direction away was. Finally her eyes latched onto a gap in the running bodies or a doorway that looked safe. She had sandals on her feet, but that didn't stop her from running like a track star. My head turned to follow her progress, too afraid to breathe until she was safe. Then I saw the policeman. Saw him, and knew they were on a collision course. If she had been a second sooner, a second faster, she would have been through the doors, and he would have found someone else. I heard myself scream something, telling her to run, or telling the policemen to stop, or just screaming. Screaming. But the full force of his body hit hers and sent her flying.

I watched her in slow motion as she spun toward me, arms and legs pinwheeling. I had time to wish that she'd trip and fall into one of the chairs in front of me, but she only brushed by one of them. Not enough to stop her, only enough to throw her off balance. Another quick stumble and she was beside me. I turned to watch her, putting out an arm to stop or even just slow her down, but too late. Our eyes met as the smooth marble wall stopped her like she hadn't been moving at all. Pain flashed on her face, and she leaned into me. I caught her in my arms, but her momentum was enough to push me to the floor. I sat down hard, my back against the wall, her head in my lap. Her face was already covered with blood that was slowly making its way into her hair and down her neck. Now that she was up close I saw details that I hadn't noticed during her panicked run. Some of her long hair had been carefully braided with beads placed here and there in a repeating pattern. She wore beaded necklaces as well, one with a polished wooden peace sign, another with a small wooden cross. Her dress had fine embroidery on the edges, and until her own blood had stained it, the pretty flower pattern had been clean and bright.

She was the opposite of the hippie with the megaphone. Maybe she was shaking an angry fist right along with the rest of them, but from the looks of her it was more likely that she had been raising a pleading peace sign. She wasn't much older than I was, maybe in her first or second year of college. It occurred to me that in a few years, I could be just like her. Putting on a nice dress, fixing my hair, and joining my friends to... to what? Get in trouble with the police? No, probably not. I didn't think that the girl had that in mind when she left for City Hall that morning.

I noticed a canvas bag over her shoulder, covered in sewn on patches. Several peace signs of course, one tie dyed, one rainbow. A heart patch, an American flag, a couple that looked like girl scout badges. There was a notebook that had fallen out of the bag. A journal maybe. When I leaned forward to slide it back in the bag, the girl's eyes fluttered and opened. A pretty blue, but with a haze in them like she was figuring out where she was and trying to remember what happened. When she did, the haze turned to panic and she tried to sit up, but she didn't get far. She winced in pain, clutching my arm weakly with one hand, and then her eyes fluttered closed again.

There was blood. Everywhere.

I remember falling off a swing when I was five or six. I bumped my forehead hard enough to split the skin. Before I could catch my breath, there seemed to be blood all over, running into my eyes, inhaled into my nose when I sniffed in sobs. My father was there instantly, holding me, comforting me, and he finally got me to calm down, explaining to me how even a small cut on the head can bleed a lot. Before I knew it, he'd stopped the bleeding with a handkerchief and a kiss.

With the hippie girl's head in my lap, I tried to remember that, but there was so much blood. Her hair was streaked with it, the top of her dress covered. Even if it was a small cut, it seemed like that much blood would need to be stopped before too long. I shifted her head slightly so it rested on my thighs instead of my hands. I pulled my sweater off, leaving wide smears of red on my shirt. Lifting the girl's head again, I found what seemed to be the source of the bleeding and held the sweater there, hoping to at least slow things down.

I don't know how much time had passed, but when I lifted my head to call for help, the scene in the lobby had changed dramatically. Most of the protesters were gone.

Any that were left were sitting in a small cluster with six or seven policemen standing in a loose circle around them. On the far side of the room, a group of people that were clearly not protesters stood talking among themselves. Mostly business suits, with a few police officers keeping them calm and answering questions. Off to their side was a clump of smaller figures. My classmates, with Mr. Flynn fluttering around them.

No one seemed to have noticed me. I called for help, screamed probably, and I heard my voice echo to the ceiling. Heads snapped in my direction, and two of the closest policemen went from a standstill to a sprint in a blink. Maybe Mr. Flynn had realized he was one student short and was already looking for me, because even though he was on the far side of the room, he was next to me a few steps ahead of the policemen. But the relief on his face turned to panic again when he saw me covered in red.

Police were on radios. They were crouched beside me, lifting the girl, checking me and checking her to figure out who was hurt. Maybe there were people hurt outside as well because paramedics burst through the doors in what felt like seconds. There was a tight circle of faces around me, and then the girl was on a stretcher. She was lifted and carried away, while a paramedic knelt in front of me, asking me questions and shining a light in my eyes. He must have decided I was fine because he was gone as quickly as he came and the corner of the lobby was once again empty except for me and Mr. Flynn.

He started to say something but stopped. He tried a few words again but stopped a second time. Instead he ended up sitting down cross-legged next to me. I moved the bag beside me to make room for him and realized that it belonged to the hippie girl, that it had been left behind when she was carried away. I pulled it toward me, wrapping the strap once around my wrist. Then I leaned my head against the wall behind me and closed my eyes.

Dark

The bus ride back to Forestville was silent, a stark contrast to the noisy, excitement filled ride down to San Francisco. Now past dark, there was little to see outside the windows, and a lot of kids slept. Mr. Flynn was in the front of the bus. He alternated between sitting and standing up, scanning the rows of students behind him. There was nothing to see, no talkers to hush, no note-passers to intercept. But he still stood up occasionally, his worried eyes touching all of us.

He'd offered me a clean shirt before we got on the bus. I have no idea where he got it. Maybe his City Hall friend. I refused. Sitting there on the bus, I didn't yet have the words to describe the way it felt, but the blood streaking my shirt and soaked into my pants had a weight to it that I didn't think I could shed just by changing clothes. Mr. Flynn reluctantly settled for sending me to the bathroom so I could wash my hands and face before he let me on the bus.

No one sat next to me on the ride home. I didn't blame them, I wouldn't have sat next to me either. And though it wasn't a conscious decision, I had put the bag I'd picked up on the seat next to me rather than setting it on my blood stained lap or on the floor at my feet.

I was glad for the empty seat. If someone was sitting there, then I'd need to make conversation. I didn't want to talk, and I didn't want to think.

Mr. Flynn left the safety of his front seat and began a slow walk toward the back of the bus. He stopped every couple seats, maybe thinking he'd be able to start a conversation with one of the students, but each stop ended in an awkward pause where Mr. Flynn could only look around again like he'd done from his seat and then eventually give up and move on.

I was sitting about halfway back and couldn't help but watch Mr. Flynn's stuttering progress, hoping he'd give up before he got close enough to me that I'd be forced to ignore him, but I eventually found myself staring at the braided hair of the girl in front of me, and hoping that the blurred Mr. Flynn in my peripheral vision would move down the aisle and leave me alone.

Unable to take it any longer, I turned to look up at him, and his eyes held mine for a second before shifting down to the seat beside me for the briefest moment and then returning to my own.

I knew what his glance meant, but stared ahead, ignoring him as long as I could, before I reached over and tugged the patch covered bag out of the seat beside me and onto my lap. Still Mr. Flynn remained standing in the aisle, uncomfortably shifting from one foot to the other, as if the now empty seat wasn't enough of an invitation. I turned again to make eye contact and mumbled an almost silent, "Sit."

He sighed and slumped into the seat, remaining silent long enough for me to hope that he was only looking for a change of scenery and his uncomfortable walk down the bus aisle was just about finding a new place to sit. He opened his mouth more than once but was unable to push any words out and finally resorted to tracing lopsided shapes on the textured vinyl of the seatback in front of us until he could find something to say.

"I... City Hall... the girl..." Even with the silence broken, Mr. Flynn seemed to be choosing words small enough to fit into the cramped air between us. "I'm sorry."

I let the dark landscape outside my window roll by while I mulled over the apology. What did Mr. Flynn have to apologize for, really? He'd set up the trip to San Francisco as a way to expose a bunch of high school kids to some opinions that were likely quite different from the ones they got at home. He'd ended up walking us into the middle of a riot scene that could have very easily gotten his students injured or killed. But I could forgive him for that. Mr. Flynn had spent most of the school year putting ideas in our heads that weren't there in September, and he had no way of knowing that the little protest outside City Hall was going to turn into something that would end up on the TV news that night. In fact, after staring at a couple miles of darkness outside, I realized I wasn't really angry at Mr. Flynn at all.

I was angry at myself. Angry for listening to the shouted slogans that stuck in my brain and made me doubt whether the war we were in was really something we should be fighting at all. At the same time, I was embarrassed for being naïve enough to think that something like a war could be so black and white, that there could be a clear right and wrong to it all, and that our country would always be on the right side.

The police had shown me how foolish I was to think that. The newspaper headlines would likely tell a slanted story of law breaking hippies, and a police force that protected everyone in City Hall. And the newspaper would be partly right. The crowds outside shouldn't have stormed into the building, and the police were right to stop them when they did. But that was the black and white version. I knew a different story, and couldn't help but question all I had blindly believed about our role in Vietnam. It was those two voices that had been arguing with each other during the long bus ride back home, filling the space around me while I sat silently alone in my seat. I finally broke my silence.

"My father's over there." The words came out of my mouth quickly.

Mr. Flynn didn't say anything. He let out a long breath, sat back far enough that his head rested against the seat, and closed his eyes. My short explanation was enough. I wasn't mad at him, wasn't angry about the danger he'd put us in. He'd done what he'd set out to do on our field trip. He'd opened my eyes. He'd shown me the reality we were in, and now the conflict of right and wrong was stuck inside me the same way it was stuck in him. But Mr. Flynn's conflict came from newspaper headlines and the nightly news, mine came from a place a little closer to home.

We sat in silence for the rest of the bus ride. During that last, long hour of the trip, we stopped being teacher and student sitting beside each other on the bus. Mr. Flynn had taught me something about the world, and at the same time, I'd shown him that our great big world for some people often boils down to a single person who is far, far away. If I'd had the chance to talk to Mr. Flynn again, I think we both would have made pretty good teachers for each other.

I guess Mr. Flynn must have made a phone call before we left City Hall because somehow it seemed like the whole town was waiting in the high school parking lot when our bus pulled in. Maybe the police in San Francisco had contacted Forestville. Maybe people had just seen it on the news. Cars clustered in the first few rows closest to the school building, and a few police cars sat askew on the edges, their flashing red and blue lights off but still catching a glint from the streetlights.

My classmates mumbled to each other as they grabbed their things and paraded off the bus. I stayed where I was, letting the kids behind me filter past while I looked out the window at students already reunited with their parents. As the last of the line teetered down the bus steps, I pulled myself out of the seat and went down the aisle.

I'd never really talked with my mother about a pickup plan. Talking to her would have meant she would have had to talk back, and that felt suspiciously like a conversation. It was irresponsible of me I guess. With no close friends in my history class, I'd still assumed I'd just find a classmate to catch a late night ride home with. But I'd sat and watched through the bus window as most of the cars silently rolled away, so that when I emerged from the bus there was only a small cluster of people, and the police cars, and my mother.

My mother.

She stood there in front of me with her mouth open like a word had been caught there between her tongue and teeth. My feet moved forward without my brain telling them to do so. There were police officers in the parking lot before I came off the bus. Mr. Flynn and the principal were there too, but now the only person my brain saw was my mother. Like my feet, my arms rose without my thinking and then fell around her.

Her body shook uncontrollably with gasps of tears so violent that mine shook as well. Then I realized that it was actually my body shaking. My tears.

"I miss him so much," I said, feeling the emotions of almost a year spill out of me in sobs. So much that there couldn't possibly be any more inside of me, until my mother said, "I miss him too."

Evening News

There was a substitute teacher in Mr. Flynn's room when we returned to school. She didn't explain why she was there or mention Mr. Flynn. She just put an assignment on the board and told us which chapter to read in the textbook. She was there the next day too. By the end of the week, we were no longer surprised when we came in the room and saw her. She was OK as far as teachers go. She learned our names, she graded our work fairly. But she didn't ask us what we thought, and she didn't answer our questions with more questions.

The one hundred photographs of famous Americans no longer hung on the walls.

Everyone at school wanted to talk about what had happened in San Francisco, and everyone who went on the trip had their own piece of the story to tell. Where they were standing, what they'd seen, what they did when the riot started. The newspapers called it a riot. It had stopped being a protest when the crowd pushed through the doors of City Hall I guess.

Kids listened to stories, and retold them, and spread them through the halls. But they were still missing my part of the story. They asked me about the "hippie girl" or the "bloody girl." When someone at my locker asked me about the "dead girl," I froze halfway through my locker combination. I'd assumed she was fine after the paramedics came. I'd assumed they carried her to an ambulance and took her to a hospital and she was fine. It didn't occur to me that she could have died. But there was a lot of blood. A lot of it.

But no one was talking about why all those people were there in the first place. No one was talking about the hippie with the megaphone and his garbled, angry words. No one was talking about why the police were called in to bust up a group of people calling for the end to a war. Mr. Flynn had taken us to the city to show us that there were crowds of people who disagreed with what was going on, people who saw things differently than the newspapers did, people who disagreed with what our government was doing, people who were willing to speak up and say that it wasn't right. And we sure saw it, saw more than Mr. Flynn ever expected us to see. But it seemed that nothing had changed in us. We'd come home with a week's worth of stories to tell, and that was that. It didn't seem right.

At home each night, I began watching the six o'clock news with my mother. There was no heart-to-heart conversation, not on the car ride home the day of the riot, not in the days that followed. Again where I expected monumental change, there was none. Except that we watched the news. Together.

The really bad news didn't make it to TV: images of the protesting monk who set himself on fire in the middle of Saigon; children crying, running down a road with a wall of fiery napalm behind them; skies thick with helicopters; and bandaged soldiers with eyes that had seen things they would never forget. Maybe those pictures showed up on the front pages of newspapers in San Francisco or Sacramento, but if we saw them at all in the *Santa Rosa Star*, they were buried in the middle section or stuck next to an opinion piece that made them seem like they weren't really news, only something that someone thought. I'd figured out though, that the real news was there if you knew where to look, and I was looking.

In the years to come, there would be more photographs, and not all of them from faraway Vietnam: the screaming woman at that little university in Ohio, kneeling over the body of a protester killed by the National Guard; the soldier returning from Vietnam, exiting the plane, falling to his knees, and kissing American ground; National Guardsmen at the Pentagon, looking confused and helpless as protesters placed flowers in the barrels of their guns.

The news anchors on our screen shared careful facts about troop movements, parts of the country that our soldiers controlled, and the President's resolve to stay until we won the war. But the filtered news was really just background noise for my mom and me while we each mulled over our thoughts. We didn't talk. We didn't need to. We both knew we were missing my father, holding our breath until he came home, and scanning the screen for a hint that would tell us he was OK.

Like having a substitute teacher in Mr. Flynn's room, sitting with my mother on the couch and watching the news eventually seemed like something that had always been, even though it had only been going on for about two weeks.

That's when my mother brought out the shoebox full of letters. It sat there on the couch between us for a while without me even wondering what it was. Just something taking up space. Until I leaned over to rest my head on my mother's shoulder and brushed my hand on it. My mother's hand was instantly on mine, and then together we were taking the lid off the box.

There, lined up in a neat row, were my father's letters. She pulled out the first envelope, slid the letter out, unfolded it, and held it out so we both could read. My father's neat handwriting described the flight over, his first days on the ground, and the adjustments of settling into a new base. And just like my father's smile shrug that said so much to me, there in all the lines I read was the message that none of the words said. "I love you. I miss you. I love you. I miss you."

I looked up at my mother, wondering if she read it that way too, or if she only saw the newsy sentences about the new base. One look and I knew she did. And if she saw it in the words on the page, she surely understood what my father was saying with his crooked smiles and half shrugs. She'd understood everything, but for some reason, she let me think that my father and I were the only ones in on the secret, that it was just the two of us with that special connection.

We read letters into the night. At first my mother held them between us for our eyes to silently scan. Eventually we took turns reading them aloud, which was better because we could laugh together at the funny parts, and then cry together because the funny parts were just in the letter and my father wasn't in the room.

Television programs blended together, and then the news was on again at 11:00, but it was still just background. We kept reading until the test pattern came on the screen and the high pitched whining sound interrupted us. I jumped up to turn the TV off, and then we read until we reached the end of the box.

The kids at school seemed to move on from the episode in San Francisco after a week or two. The stories died down, and they found other happenings to catch their interest. But I got tired of not talking about what Mr. Flynn was trying to show us, and I had enough of the substitute. I raised my hand when she asked a question, and when she called on me I had a question of my own.

"Where's Mr. Flynn?"

Her expression stumbled and she snapped out, "I beg your pardon?"

"Where's Mr. Flynn?"

"Young lady..."

"Elizabeth. Mr. Flynn always called us by name," I said and then added, "Why is he not here?" Reaction in the classroom was mixed. Some kids simply grinned or laughed at one of their classmates interrupting the teacher and disrupting the lesson. Others looked at me with surprised faces or rolled their eyes and shook their heads. I only noticed a few nodding their heads in agreement or mumbling their own questions about Mr. Flynn's absence.

The substitute had overcome the surprise of my question and composed herself. "Mr. Flynn was removed from this classroom because his lessons and teaching were not in line with the ideals of the school or this community," she said in a voice that sounded rehearsed, like she was just repeating a line the principal had given her if the students ever asked.

"What ideals?" I snapped back. "What did he teach us that was wrong? He didn't do anything against the school or the town. He was only trying to show us…"

This time it was my turn to get interrupted. "Mr. Flynn endangered his students and exposed them to anti-American opinions." I couldn't tell if she was still reciting practiced lines fed to her by the principal, but her face made it easy to see she agreed wholeheartedly with what she was saying. Either way she sounded like a page from our history book.

"Are you talking about the war? Vietnam? Protesting the war? Is that what you mean by anti-American? Not wanting a war is anti-American?" I was peppering the substitute with questions, no longer waiting for her answers or letting her interrupt, and then my eyes darted around and I was asking questions to the room. "He was trying to show us other opinions. Don't you see that? What's wrong with listening to other ideas? How do we know we should be fighting this war? How do we know it's right?" I had stood up without realizing it, and my hands were clenched.

The faces on my classmates were changing. The kids who had been laughing before were no longer smiling, some looking out the window or bent down over their books. The ones who had been nodding before were gesturing for me to sit down or to be quiet, the closer ones hissing whispers. "Bethy, enough already." and "Don't say that stuff, Bethy." The eye rollers' faces had turned angry and their shouts drowned out the last of my questions. I was silenced and could only look around the room at kids who I thought were just like me, unable to see how they could have a reaction so different from mine. The bell to end class saved me.

Kids grabbed their books and pushed for the door. I was bumped a few times more than what seemed normal, and some kids grumbled comments as they brushed past. "My father's over there. You saying he's doing something wrong?" and "Anti-American." As I squeezed through the door, the last comment I heard stuck with me long after I left the classroom and found myself walking alone down the hallway. "I just want to forget that day."

The kids with family fighting in the war I understood. I was still trying to figure out how my father, who always did everything right, could be a part of a war that now seemed so wrong. And I had spent enough time listening to Mr. Johnson over the top of his paper to know that it was pretty common for people to see opinions against the war as unpatriotic and un-American. But the realization that some kids might just want to forget everything that had happened in San Francisco churned in me. Did they want to forget because what had happened was frightening? Or were the conflicting opinions of right and wrong too much to think about, so that it was easier to just not think about it at all and try to forget the whole thing? After spending weeks wrestling with my own conflicting feelings and waking up from more than a few dreams that had me back in a pushing shoving crowd or trying to wipe blood from my hands, I could see how forgetting the protest and all that followed could be the easiest thing to do. But I had two reminders that kept me thinking about it.

The hippie girl's bag with the journal hung from the back of a chair in my room, slightly off kilter like it would probably have hung if it were on her shoulder. Digging through the bag didn't feel right, but since the journal was big enough that a corner stuck out of the bag, I felt OK pulling it out. I didn't read it, but I'd pull it out most nights, look at the cover with its curly-cue lines encircling peace signs, and then I'd open the cover and look at the neat handwriting on the inside cover.

Emmie Hatcher
1461 Page Street
San Francisco

I wondered about Emmie Hatcher, wondered what her story was before getting shoved into that wall. It didn't feel right reading her journal though. Journals are private – it was hers and hers only. But at the same time, I didn't want to let it go. I couldn't let it go. I needed it, just like I needed the bag's peace symbols, smiley faces, and rainbow patches. So the bag hung there on the back of my chair holding the journal's secrets inside.

The other reminder was balled up in the back corner of my closet, my white t-shirt covered in Emmie's blood. I knew it would never come clean, but it didn't seem like something that should just get thrown out, and I knew my mother would throw it out if she saw it. I had tossed it into the closet the night we came home, and there it stayed. It was there waiting in the corner, every time I opened my closet to find something to wear.

Gravity

I hadn't shown Miss E. my twenty words yet. I meant to. I'd planned on showing them to her before I turned them into Mr. Flynn. But the words I ended up with were not what I'd expected when I started. And then San Francisco happened, and for a while, I had other things on my mind, and Mr. Johnson told me I should take a little time at home. I knew I didn't need the excuse of grocery deliveries to visit Miss E. anymore, so when I finally got around to admitting to myself that taking time off from Johnson's store was actually my excuse for not visiting, I knew it was time.

I could hear the engines while riding past the farm next to Miss E.'s. I suppose someone who wasn't expecting to hear a forty-year-old airplane turning over its engines every month or so would just assume it was farm machinery of some kind. But the roar was unmistakable by the time I reached the top of the small hill that overlooked her farm and coasted my bike down the last stretch of dirt driveway. I covered my ears, helplessly trying to block it out.

The door to the barn was wide open, but I stood off to one side straddling my bike, waiting, listening. I thought about just turning around and leaving. Miss E. hadn't seen me yet and certainly wouldn't hear me biking away. I put my foot on the pedal to go, but stopped. This was either the worst time to show her what I'd written or the best. I figured I'd better stick around to find out which.

The engines finally sputtered to a stop and the barn was once again silent, frozen in time again. I replayed the time we sat in the cockpit, my ears still ringing and Miss E. still staring out the window. One minute. And then the time it took us to crawl back out of the plane. Another minute. And then the slow circle around, touching the wing tips, the tail, the propeller blades. Another minute.

And there was Miss E. emerging from the dark stillness of the barn. She didn't see me at first and had one door closed and was pushing the other when she looked up. If she was surprised to see me, there was nothing in her that betrayed it.

"Was wondering when you'd make it out again." My mouth opened with nothing in it, but Miss E. saved me the effort of looking for words. "Heard you had some trouble down there in the city. You OK?" She didn't wait for my answer, and instead bent her weight into closing the door again.

I hopped off my bike and dug the paper out of my back pocket while I trotted to the spot where the doors would meet and then stood there in the way. Miss E. had the door moving with enough inertia that she had to lean backwards and dig her heels in to stop it before it hit me.

"Good way to get yourself..." she started in surprise but stopped when I thrust the paper toward her.

"No more closing the door." Then it was Miss E.'s turn to stand with mouth open and nothing to say, until I shook the paper and she took it.

I watched her eyes the way I'd done with Mr. Flynn, running the words through my head and guessing what line she was on. Her eyes narrowed when I thought they would and I noticed the paper crinkle a little as she held it tighter. Miss E.'s eyes flicked up at me once and I forced myself to look back, resisting the urge to drop them to the ground. She'd gotten to the end. Her eyes jumped up and down like she was picking out individual lines, and I knew she'd found the ones that really said what I wanted to say, the lines that told her secret.

I realized then that I'd never seen Miss E. angry, not in town when she walked by the silent staring people, not when she watched me knock out Peter Anderson in front of the library, not when her airplane's engine died a thousand feet above the ground. But when the hand that was resting on the heavy locking hasp of the barn door slammed it into the wood with a piecing clank, Miss E's eyes jumped from the paper up to mine and the anger in them was unmistakable.

She was twenty steps away from me before I realized she'd turned. She walked right into the tall grass of the field at a surprising pace, fast enough that I had to jog to catch up.

"Miss E," I called after her, but she didn't stop. "Miss E!" still trying to keep up. I thought about stopping, just letting her go. Would I just stand there and wait for her to come back? Would I get back on my bike and leave? "Amelia! What are you afraid of?" I called instead.

She whirled on me so fast I nearly ran into her before I could stop. "You think I'm afraid? Afraid!" I'd also never heard Miss E. yell before. "Afraid of flying that plane that I've flown all over the world? Afraid of those people in town?" At that she looked down at the paper in her hand and paused long enough that I thought maybe she'd said all she wanted to, and then she looked back up and shook the paper at me. "How dare you! Who did you show this to? Who knows? Who did you tell about me?"

With that question, she must have seen the confusion on my face. The angry eyes were gone, but the expression that replaced them wasn't one I'd seen before, not the wise eyes that knew the answer and made me figure it out for myself, or the twinkling eyes I'd seen after she had started up the Electra. This was something else.

Miss E.'s face worked in fits and starts. She'd start to say a word and then stop and look around like she was searching for the next one. She shifted the paper from one hand to the other, clenching the hand that had just passed it off, like it hurt to hold it. Then finally her hands came together to crumple the paper between them, and as she did, Miss E. seemed to crumple herself, until she ended up sitting on the ground with her face between her knees.

I thought about our afternoon in the cornfield, me left sitting on the picnic blanket still stinging from the conversation we'd just had about my mother, and Miss E. hopping up to go work on the plane like we'd been talking about nothing more important than the weather. I thought about how she jumped out of conversations and moved to the next subject without ever acknowledging the dodge, and how it annoyed me until I realized on our way back to the air strip that she probably did it to give me time to think and figure things out for myself. I thought about doing the same to her. Or was it *for* her? I thought about just walking back to the barn, back to my bike, and leaving Miss E. to her thoughts in the tall grass. Instead, I sat down next to her.

I spent a few minutes nervously shifting on the lumpy ground waiting for Miss E. to respond. Then I started to feel awkward about where I'd sat, a comfortable distance that respected personal space, but under the present circumstances, it felt far away. I scooted closer, and then again. After feeling a little like we were lined up on bleachers waiting for a baseball game to spring up in the field ahead of us, I shuffled myself through a turn and sat with my back to Miss E.

"If you're done square dancing, Bets, you might consider leaning back so we can both relax a bit." After minutes of silence, the sudden voice made me jump a little, but I relaxed again and leaned back as Miss E. did the same so we could use each other as a back rest. We sat like that long enough for me to stop wondering about what Miss E. was going to say and start drifting into my own thoughts. I watched a cloud move in from the east and let my eyes track it as it moved over us and then away toward the horizon. I thought about the ocean between me and my father and wondered if it was possible for him to see the same cloud.

"Clouds are funny, Bets. They look all white and fluffy from the ground, but you get up in them and it's like day turned to night, the green far below and the endless blue above fade to a flat, heavy grey all around. It makes perfect sense, watching those acres of white float along like nothing, to think they don't weigh anything, like gravity doesn't exist for them. But when you're in the middle of one, they seem heavy like a stone." With the last sentence I felt Miss E. tense, and I waited for the pause to end.

"Gravity, Bets. You're always fighting it in the air, doing everything you can to make a bunch of metal behave like it belongs in the sky with those clouds instead of stuck on the ground. Air speed, wind direction, prop angle, flaps, ailerons, throttle, fuel mixture, you name it, it all adds up to keeping something in the air that really has no business being there. They all work together to fight gravity. Seemed like some places had extra gravity when I was flying, like the place was doing everything it could to pull me down out of the air. Places wouldn't let me leave the ground some days. People would say I was carrying too much fuel or that the mountain air was too thin. But it all comes down to gravity. It does its best to keep things where they belong, and lets us break the rules from time to time if we put the pieces together just right.

"But the gravity here is different, Bets. I've let it have too many years of pulling on me. Gravity will do that if you let it, staying in one place too long. You start out with a little excuse and a little bit of time. I'll just stay here a few months, till I get my thoughts sorted out, you say. But a few months add up to a year, and if you stayed one year you might as well stay two. And two years go so fast you don't even have time to think, so two becomes five. And before you know it you start thinking you might never leave, and wondering why you ever wanted to, and you keep making excuses for staying, until you realize you've waited so long there's nothing left to leave for."

With that, Miss E. pulled herself from the ground. Maybe it was from sitting too long, or maybe it was me finally noticing her real age, but it seemed to me she had to fight gravity to get up. She turned toward me, and I leaned back on my hands and tilted my head to see her face under the mop of hair tossing in the light breeze.

"I've got no business being angry at you, Bets. I hope you'll forgive an old lady her crankiness. You didn't do anything wrong by writing what you did. You did a fine job of sneaking in the truth without letting anyone in on our secret. And I know these words are meant to get an old lady moving again. I've known for a long time, Bets, but was afraid to admit it. I'm stuck on this farm. But it isn't those boys in the control tower over at Oakland that are keeping me here, and it's not the reporters waiting to crowd me with a bunch of hullabaloo when I land. I'm stuck because I'm afraid of what happens next. What happens when no one cares? What happens when the world decides the story of Amelia Earhart disappearing over the ocean is a heck of a lot more interesting than her growing old on a middle-of-nowhere farm? What happens when they all laugh at the crazy old lady claiming to be Amelia Earhart?"

She walked away without another word and disappeared back toward the barn. I took a step to follow her before I noticed the crumpled white paper in the grass. Miss E.'s twenty words. I picked them up, smoothed the paper against my thigh, folded it, and slid it into my back pocket.

Letters

I parked my bike in front of the library after school the next day. The librarian looked a little surprised when she saw me. After a constant stream of biography-hunting ninth graders, the library had turned into a peaceful recluse in comparison. I lifted a hand in greeting and pulled my backpack strap farther up on my shoulder as if to indicate that I was there for school business. She dropped her eyes and went back to stamping due dates on book inserts.

I found my way to the biography section and ran my fingers along the book spines, reciting the alphabet backwards working my way toward the E's. The book I was looking for was easy to find – it had been on my desk long enough that I recognized the color and lettering. I pulled it from the shelf and walked back toward the checkout desk. Even though the librarian had no way of knowing what I had planned for the book, I felt guilty. She slipped in one of the due date cards she'd been stamping and then flipped the book over to look at the cover.

"Pity about that Earhart woman," she said, not bothering to lift her eyes to look at me. "We were ready for a celebration being so close to her takeoff and landing spot. I suppose all that's left of her now is in the history books, huh?" She slid the book along the desk toward me as if to punctuate her point and then turned back to her work.

I left the library slowly, thinking about what Miss E. had said the day before and wondering how the woman behind the desk would react to Amelia Earhart's return. I walked down Front Street with the same thought in mind, glancing at the people who passed me on the sidewalk and gauging what their reaction might be.

I hadn't really thought about it until the librarian mentioned it, but the older people in town were probably living in the area when Miss E. made her world flight. They might even have driven down to Oakland to watch her take off or made plans to watch her land. For them, finding out that Amelia Earhart was still alive and living just outside of town would be pretty exciting, like that celebration they were ready for but never had. But for most of the town, those people who were my parents' age or younger, and the kids like me, Amelia Earhart was just someone from the history books, like the librarian had said. Would we give her any more attention than we gave our history books?

These new thoughts made me even more resolved to see my plan through. I walked a block or two from the library. I suppose I could have taken care of things right there on one of the benches in front of the library building, but it didn't feel right. I ended up on a bench near the bulletin board where the outdated yard-sale flyer still hung. The Chevy had either sold or the owner had decided it ran so great that it was worth keeping. I sat there for a few minutes watching people walk by before I opened the book. I flipped to the middle and found the page that I knew was there, the page that folded out into a full sized map of Amelia Earhart's route around the world. Then I tugged at it gently until its edge pulled free from the pages on either side. I gradually tore the page out, careful to get it all and not leave any torn edges behind. When I was finished, no evidence of the extra map page remained between pages 57 and 58, and someone checking out the book after me would never guess that it had been there.

I dug through my backpack for a pen and then, I drew a thin black line from Howland Island in the Pacific diagonally up to Hawaii and then farther still to Oakland, California. And then, in block all-caps print as neat as I could manage, I wrote a sentence that followed the route with the bottoms of the letters not quite touching the line I'd just drawn, then underlined two of the words.

WHY DO <u>YOU</u> CARE WHAT <u>THEY</u> THINK?

I bought an envelope and stamp at the post office and wrote the address I knew by heart. The map had been folded to fit the size of the book, and I had to unfold and refold a couple of times before I got it to fit flat in the envelope. I dropped my letter in the mailbox on my way out of the post office, and then, as a gesture that completed my task entirely, I walked back to the library and let the Amelia Earhart book, now one page thinner, slide into the book deposit slot outside the main doors.

Three days later, a letter arrived for me. Although I checked the mailbox when I arrived home from school most days, I didn't normally get mail. I always just brought in the mail for my mother, most days not even looking at what it was, unless there was a letter from my father. Other than a few birthday cards from aunts and uncles I'd never met, I couldn't remember ever having seen an envelope addressed to me. I would have put the letter on the kitchen counter like I did any other day, except that I noticed the crossed out address and was curious enough to take a look.

There in my handwriting was Miss E.'s address, crossed out, and then written below it in a much neater script was my name and below that my own address. I hadn't bothered writing a return address; I figured Miss E. would know who the letter had come from. Miss E. hadn't bothered either.

I slipped a finger inside the envelope and tore it open. Reaching in I could tell there was more in there than a letter, and by the time I had it only partially pulled out I realized it was a map. But it wasn't my map. That was easy to see right away. Not a world map. No oceans, no continents. Mostly streets laid out in a grid pattern, rimmed by water. San Francisco.

And toward the top right of the map, was a circle of red ink. I had to look closely to see what was at its center. City Hall. Next to the circle in the same red ink and the same neat script that adorned the envelope were three words, the third one underlined.

WHY DO <u>YOU</u>?

Protest

I spent the evening reading Emmie Hatcher's journal.

Well, I didn't really read it. Not all the pages. Not all the words. I'd already made up my mind that the journal was off limits. But I skimmed it. I looked for answers. I wanted to know why Emmie ended up where she did on that day in San Francisco. What made her decide to come to City Hall? What caused her to run into the building when the police came, instead of running away like some on the fringes of the crowd had done? Why was Emmie pulled into the fire? Or had she thrown herself in?

She was only a few years older than me. She seemed like someone I could share a pizza with at Sonny's, and I guessed that if we flipped through each other's record albums, we'd find a lot of duplicates. But until my trip to San Francisco, I didn't even know there was anything to protest about. So how did a person go from innocent high school student to Vietnam War protester in just a few years? Plus, there was another question I wanted answered, and I was pretty sure if I found the answer to that one, all the others would fall into place.

On Emmie's bag, there was a small American flag. Lots of people had flag patches. They sewed them onto everything right next to their peace signs. But Emmie's was different. I knew right where it came from, and it had no business being on her bag. Emmie's flag belonged on a United States Army uniform.

When I was still small enough to sit on my father's lap, he would show me each of the emblems on his uniform and explain what they were: the ones that showed his rank, the ones he'd received for special honors, and the flag. The flag was my favorite, and after he was finished, I'd rest my head on his shoulder and try to count the tiny stars.

So Emmie's flag could have come from her father's uniform, or maybe an older brother's. It crossed my mind that it could be a boyfriend's, but most boys Emmie's age were going out of their way to avoid going to Vietnam, they certainly weren't volunteering. It didn't really matter who the flag came from though. I'd seen how my father took care of his uniform. He'd have my mother fix buttons that seemed perfectly fine to me. He wouldn't leave the house until it was perfect, and I'd been on base and knew he wasn't the only one. So the only way Emmie would get an American Flag off of someone's uniform was if the person wasn't wearing it anymore, and I had a pretty good guess why.

So I skimmed her journal. I found the answers I was looking for, and I decided what I needed to do next.

The day El Molino High School held the pep rally, I wore a sweatshirt to school. I would have been more comfortable without it, but the day wasn't so warm that I stood out wearing it. During the entire school day, I don't think anyone even noticed me. That was the point.

The pep rally was scheduled for the last hour of the day. Teachers grumbled about it in most of my classes because they'd skimmed minutes off each period so we'd end up going to all our classes but finish with time left in the school day for the rally. While they used up precious minutes writing on the chalkboard or passing out papers, teachers mumbled things like "No time for instruction" or "Disrupts the flow of my lesson."

The football players and cheerleaders were all wearing their uniforms, and they were chattering between classes and at lunch about what would be happening at the rally. Most kids just thought it was cool to have shorter classes.

After the last class of the day, students tossed books in lockers and started flowing into the gym. I walked faster than others, squeezing around and between, until I got to the double doors leading into the gym. I had a brief memory of San Francisco as the people in front slowed to get through the doors while the people behind kept closing in. I pushed aside the memory and squeezed through the door. I wanted a good seat.

I ended up in the third row of the center section of bleachers. I was in plain view of the kids on the opposite side of the gym, and if I stood up the kids behind me couldn't help but see me. My seat was perfect for what I had in mind.

We'd had a rally in the fall before a big football game, and another halfway through the school year when the basketball team had nearly made it to regionals, but no one was entirely sure who we were rallying for today. The guys on the football and basketball teams all sat together, and they seemed to have come in as a group with their arms raised and smiles on their faces after most of the other students had been seated, but they tended to do that anyway, traveling the halls in groups and coming into class last minute so they could be seen by everyone. The school had a baseball team, but they were struggling to get on base, let alone fill the bleachers. I guess if anyone needed the student body to rally behind them, the baseball team did.

The principal spoke briefly, reminding students to behave themselves and demonstrate self-control, even if they were brimming with school pride. Then he passed the microphone over to Miss Hess, the English teacher in charge of the student counsel. She was flanked on either side by the class president and vice president, two seniors whose names I didn't know even though I think they'd managed to introduce themselves to everyone in the cafeteria while elections were going on.

I shifted in my seat, waiting for the right moment. Half the kids on the bleachers were talking or nodding off, so I needed something that would at least keep their attention for a little while. I fiddled with the zipper on my sweatshirt and thumbed the corner of the notebook on my lap. When a blare of horns and the thump of a drum caused an audible gasp, I knew the time had come.

The marching band was coming in through the two sets of double doors. Two lines through each door merged into a column of four that stepped rhythmically toward the other side of the gym and then turned in unison to face away from the students on my side and then toward them. The space around us was filled with their slightly tuneless rendition of the school fight song. Conversation was impossible and many an afternoon nap was cut short. It was time.

I stood up.

I unzipped my sweatshirt, shook it from my shoulders, and let it slide off my arms and drop onto my seat, revealing the white t-shirt I'd worn to San Francisco, still covered in Emmie Hatcher's blood. I flipped my notebook open to the spot with the folded over corner, the one where I had written the words "NO WAR" in dark capital letters on one page and then again on the facing page. Folding the notebook completely open, I ended up with a two-sided sign. I held it over my head so it could be seen by the students across the gym as well as those behind me, then I stepped up onto my seat just to be sure everyone could see me.

At first the only reaction came from the students around me. Those on either side leaning away from me and craning their necks to figure out what the heck I was doing. Then a few shouts from behind, "Hey!" and "Down in front!" Then the pointing started on the other side of the gym. It was like a ripple on water. Someone would point, elbow the person next to them, and then point at me again. Then it would carry on with the next person, left and right, up and down.

The crowd on my side couldn't see my bloody t-shirt, just my sign, and those on the sides couldn't even see that. But they could see the reaction on the other side of the gym, and students in the bleachers beside me were flowing down to the gym floor to get a better look.

The band was too focused on their performance to notice anything. They marched on, blaring out their tune, until teachers who had been checking their watches and shifting their weight from foot to foot seconds ago realized what was going on and ran out with arms waving in a downward motion like they were pushing the sound of the instruments to the floor. Horns squeaked and drums rattled to a stop, while some marchers, their eyes focused on the music in front of them ran into others. There was a split second of near silence before the murmuring voices grew to a crescendo.

Teachers became sheepherders, trying to direct a crowd of students out of the gym when all they wanted to do was gawk at me. The principal's head snapped from side to side. He shouted at students, he shouted at teachers, he waved his arms as if signaling to a plane landing on an aircraft carrier.

No one thought to run up to me, pull the notebook out of my hands, and wrap my sweatshirt around me. Instead they shooed students out of the gym as if it were filled with something contagious. But really, that's exactly what I was hoping for. I had something that I needed everyone to catch.

From where I sat in the principal's office, I could see out the window and watch as students piled on buses to leave school. There were some juniors and seniors who drove themselves, and some kids who lived close enough to walk. In less than ten minutes, the sidewalks and bus loop in front of school were empty and silent. I had been asked to stay.

I'd also been asked to put on my gym clothes. When I dropped it on her desk, Mrs. Hutcheson, the principal's secretary, had picked up my shirt by hooking her pen inside the collar. She promptly dropped it into the waste-basket beside her desk, and then carried the wastebasket at arm's length as she ushered me into the principal's office. She left the wastebasket in the chair beside me and left the room in a huff. My notebook sat on the principal's desk, tastefully closed.

Mr. Higgins, the principal, had walked me to the main office from the gym after a voice on the PA had instructed students to return to their last period classroom and the halls were slowly cleared. Maybe teachers would be pleased to be getting some instructional time back, although I was hoping most of the students would be talking about what they saw in the gym, and teachers would have their work cut out for them just getting kids to settle down. He left me with Mrs. Hutcheson and grumbled something about needing to be out in the hallways to monitor dismissal and not having the time to deal with troublemakers. I figured with the front of school clearing out, he'd be joining me in his office soon.

Like I had imagined Miss E. going through the routine of exiting her plane and circling it before she left the barn, I mentally counted down the time it would take Mr. Higgins to walk down the hallway from the school lobby where he normally stood during dismissal, enter the front office, and then join me at his desk. I wondered after I got down to zero and was still alone, but then I heard quiet voices outside the door: Mr. Higgins loud and clear, but not in the same tone he'd used with me; Mrs. Hutcheson, barely audible, "Yes, of course." And there was a third voice, one I'd been expecting.

When Mr. Higgins entered his office, my mother was at his side. He walked quickly over to the chair next to me and moved the wastebasket to the floor so she could sit beside me. Then just as quickly, he moved behind his desk and planted himself in his chair. My mother sat down next to me without making eye contact.

Mr. Higgins wasted no time. "Mrs. Wells, I called you here this afternoon because... well, Elizabeth, would you like to tell your mother why you're here, or should I?"

I wrinkled my nose at the way he said my name. I was used to my mother calling me Elizabeth, and my teachers. But hearing Mr. Higgins use my full name grated on me, like he was doing it on purpose to emphasize the fact that I was in trouble.

But worse than calling me by my full name, Mr. Higgins had made the classic authority figure mistake. He'd given up his authority. By giving me the option of telling my mother what I'd done, he lost control of the story. Adults thought they were putting you on the spot, like it was some punishment to look a parent in the eye and tell them what you'd done. Maybe so, if you were out at night knocking over mailboxes or sneaking into backyard pools. But if you hadn't done anything wrong, if you had done something you felt was right, something you'd decided needed to be done, where was the shame in that? So instead of listening to Mr. Higgins catalog all the school rules I'd broken and explain how I'd been a bad influence on the other students, I turned to my mother and told her what I'd done.

"I wore the shirt that was covered in blood from the girl who'd been hit by the police when I went on the field trip to the riot in San Francisco." Mr. Higgins was instantly flustered, and I understood why. I'd put the blame on the police who hit the girl and the school for taking me to a riot scene. In my version of the story, all I'd done was wear my t-shirt to school.

"Well, Elizabeth, let's get our facts straight. You wore the shirt for the sole purpose of disrupting the pep rally and drawing attention to an unfortunate incident. An incident I might add that resulted in the prompt dismissal of the teacher responsible." Mr. Higgins seemed to be speaking without taking a breath, his voice getting higher and faster as he pressed on. "Not only did we have to end the pep rally early, but I'll now need to send a letter home to every student's parents explaining the incident and making it clear that you standing up wearing the shirt and holding a war protest sign was not a scheduled part of the rally and that the school in no way supports..."

My mother put her hand up and Mr. Higgins's voice stopped instantly. It's a good thing. He seemed to be running out of air. He sat, mouth open, looking at my mother, frozen as if the breath he'd kept himself from taking while he was talking was now stuck in his throat.

"Mr. Higgins, is your father currently serving in Vietnam?" my mother said in a low even voice.

He stammered, still holding in the breath.

"Your son or brother perhaps?"

More stammering, still no breath. Mr. Higgins was turning red in the face, either from embarrassment or lack of oxygen.

"Do you think, Mr. Higgins, that if you did have a family member serving in Vietnam, that you would perhaps want that war to end? And that instead of shouting and clapping for a football team or a group of cheerleaders, that you might want your classmates, and their principal, to at least acknowledge that many sons and fathers and brothers in this community are currently risking their lives while serving their country." Mr. Higgins finally let his breath out and seemed to deflate into his desk chair.

I had spent my time during dismissal preparing my arguments. Even the sentence I'd said when Mr. Higgins made the mistake of letting me talk first had been rehearsed and replayed in my mind. I was ready to defend myself and stand up for what I'd done. And I thought I might be able to win over my mother. But I wasn't expecting this.

My mother stood up, and Mr. Higgins practically fell out of his chair trying to do the same. Now able to see into the wastebasket, my mother gestured toward it and asked in the same steady voice, "Is that my daughter's shirt?" Mr. Higgins' face went from red to white. He nearly jumped into the wastebasket himself trying to quickly pull the shirt out. He offered it to my mother, and then glancing quickly down and realizing he was handing her a bloody piece of clothing that had just been in the garbage, he pulled it back toward himself, briefly held it out toward me, and then started looking around for something to put the shirt in. I saved him the agony and just took it from him.

We walked out of Mr. Higgins's office and passed Mrs. Hutcheson without a word. My mother stood silently behind me while I gathered some of my things from my locker. The silence continued as we walked through the halls, and I started to wonder if my mother was truly angry with me, in spite of her coming to my defense just minutes ago. Then as we exited the school building, my mother did something she hadn't done in a long time. She smiled at me.

Calling

My mother let me stay home from school the next day, which was probably the exact punishment that Mr. Higgins was going to dish out. But since it wasn't a suspension imposed by the principal, and instead was a decision made by my mother, she felt it was perfectly appropriate. I never really understood suspension. It was like something schools invented after corporal punishment was no longer allowed because they couldn't really figure out what else to do with kids who'd crossed way over the line, and they really just wanted to get them out of the school building so they didn't cause any more trouble.

To me it was all the same. It was a day off of school. But I realized after I'd had breakfast and flipped through a few pages of the newspaper without finding anything interesting, that I didn't really have any idea what I was going to do with the day. My mother had weekly lunch plans with her bridge club, and this week was her turn to host. So in a few hours, the house would be full of women, probably asking me questions about San Francisco and then turning to friends to share their opinion on what was wrong with all those hippies without ever listening to what I had to say. And eventually they'd ask why I wasn't in school.

I'd decided before my cereal was soggy that I needed to get out of the house, but anyone I would normally meet up with was in school. I could bike to town, but any adult who saw me would want to know why I wasn't in school, same as my mother's friends. So riding my bike to Miss E.'s became my only option, although once I had made the decision, it seemed like the obvious choice anyway. We hadn't left on the best of terms last time I saw her, and sending letters was clearly not the way we did business. Besides, I had news to share, and I was certain that the conversation would require nothing less than tomato juice and a seat at Miss E.'s kitchen table.

I cleaned up my breakfast dishes and told my mother that I was headed to town. She started to say something about people in town wondering why I wasn't in school, and I told her I'd be fine. Then she said something about how nice it would be for some of the ladies in the bridge club to meet me, but our screen door was already slamming. My mother had redeemed herself in many ways over the last month, but when it came to understanding a fifteen-year-old's perspective on bridge club, she still had a lot to learn.

I had pulled my bike from around the side of the house and was already throwing my leg over it, when I saw the red pickup truck rolling down the road. My first thought was surprise that Miss E. was visiting someone who lived in my neighborhood. I knew she drove to and from town, and I was with her when she drove out to Fred Noonan's airfield. I actually felt a pang of jealousy when it dawned on me that there could be another high school kid who Miss E. had gotten to know and visited when I wasn't delivering her groceries.

Then I realized the extent of my stupidity. Miss E. was coming to visit me. Or if she wasn't, and just happened to be driving by, she was going to see me standing half over my bike with my jaw drooping down to the handlebars practically. The thought of my mother poking her head out the front door to see who had pulled into the driveway and then walking out on the porch to meet Miss E. was enough to make me consider diving under a bush.

But it was inevitable. I heard the ticking engine of the pickup slow, and the wheels crunched onto the gravel of our driveway. I remembered the first time I'd seen the red pickup and how I was afraid the truck and the woman inside of it would pull me back in time. I thought about sitting at Amelia Earhart's kitchen table, climbing into her Electra, and taking a ride with her in the duster. I imagine if most of the folks in town knew what I'd been doing, they'd figure it was just about the same thing as going back in time.

The red pickup rolled to a halt, and Miss E. leaned out of the open driver's side window. She lifted her head in the same sort of funny upward nod she had given me the day I knocked out Peter Anderson. But it meant more now. The nod was like a silent hello that seemed both a lazy substitute for actually saying the word, and at the same time a closer more personal greeting, one that only I could hear. Then the driver's side door swung open, and Miss E. stepped onto the gravel driveway.

"Seems like a good day for a drive, Bets. You have any commitments?" I thought about my mother's bridge game and about town, empty of everyone other than adults. I had already decided who I wanted to spend the day with before the pickup showed up in front of my house, and here she was standing in my driveway. I shook my head, no. No commitments.

"Well then, I suppose we should spend the day rolling around. Get your things, Bets, and tell your mother you're going. We'll have packs of fun." I didn't know what things she meant for me to get, and "rolling around" didn't sound like we'd had a particular destination, but I asked anyway.

"Where we going, Bets? Well, I suppose you have some things you need to return to San Francisco. It's been awhile since I've been to the city. I thought it might be time to stop back."

San Francisco. So getting my things meant Emmie Hatcher's bag and her journal. I had long ago stopped wondering how Miss E. just seemed to know things that she really had no way of knowing, like how I'd be home on a day when every other kid was in school or that I'd been hiding someone else's things in my room for weeks.

I rushed back through the front door and into my room. I hadn't really thought about it until Miss E.'s invitation, but I knew that I couldn't keep Emmie's things forever. She might have ended up in the hospital for a day or so, but it wasn't like she had died and left me her things. And I knew who they belonged to. She wasn't just some nameless girl I'd run into. Well, she ran into me, I guess. I knew her name. I had an address. I needed her bag and journal, I think. I needed to see the bag hanging on my closet doorknob every night, as a reminder, or maybe I would have turned out like the other kids in school, just moving on without doing or saying anything. And I needed Emmie's journal, at least parts of it, to start me thinking, really thinking.

But it was time for them to go back to Emmie. I'd put the journal back in her bag, and both were hanging on the doorknob. It never really crossed my mind that Emmie would be wondering about her stuff. I had no idea what else was in the bag, but the journal alone would have been a big loss. Had she been wondering about them all this time? Checking with the police or going back to City Hall? Maybe asking friends who were there that day? Something told me no. The same way I felt like I needed to have her stuff around for a while to get me on the right track, I had a feeling that Emmie was OK with her stuff being gone temporarily.

I ran back out of my room with the bag over my shoulder and looked around for my mother. The house wasn't really that big. With a sinking feeling I realized where she was, and took slow steps toward the front door.

My mother was standing on the front porch. She'd just finished saying something and Miss E. was nodding.

Both turned to me when I opened the door and oddly, both were smiling.

"Ahh, Bets. Was wondering when you were going to make it back out here. Your mother has been good enough to keep me company while I waited." Miss E. tilted her head once toward the pickup as if to say get in, and then she opened her door and did just that. When the door slammed, my mother turned to me.

"Well, Elizabeth, don't keep her waiting. We've had a lovely chat, but I really do need to get ready for my bridge club, and you'll never get to San Francisco and back if you don't leave soon." With that she turned and disappeared into the house.

People were pretty trusting of each other when we were living around the base. Everyone knew everyone else, and being in a small town was pretty much the same. But no one knew Miss E. She was the strange lady who lived out beyond the edge of town and only showed up after she'd been gone long enough to make everybody start to wonder if she was still alive. I knew Miss E. I was comfortable getting into her truck and leaving for the day with her. But what was my mother thinking? I was tempted to head back into the house and argue with her about how irresponsible she was being, but instead I climbed into Miss E.'s red pickup truck.

"What in the world did you say to my mother to convince her to let me go with you?" There was silence from the other side of the truck cab as we bounced along a neighborhood street and then through a potholed corner and onto the main road. "Does she know? Did you tell her?"

Then after a silence long enough that I was getting ready to ask again, "Sometimes Bets, two women can have a private conversation. Your mother and I talked, and she understands the importance of our little trip today. And that's all."

"But did you..." I was cut off.

"Bets, do you really think that me telling your mother who I am and explaining why I've been hiding away would support our case for going to San Francisco?" Now there was silence on my side of the cab while the logic behind that sunk in. "Sometimes being open and honest about a thing is all it takes, Bets. You certainly wouldn't expect me to drive away with you and be gone all day without your mother knowing where we were going." We drove a mile in silence before she finished her thought. "But some lines need not be crossed."

Haight-Ashbury

The ride to San Francisco with Miss E. was the opposite of the bus ride I'd had a month earlier. It was quiet. There was very little talking, mostly the hum of the wheels on the road. No excited voices, no anticipation of what was ahead. Now and then Miss E. would comment on something we were passing or gesture toward a distant hill that had caught her eye. But mostly we were each lost in our own thoughts.

I had only ever driven with Miss E. when we went to the airstrip to fly the duster. Most of those roads were narrow and bumpy, and I blamed the roads for the ride we'd had. The ride to San Francisco made me realize the roads were merely innocent bystanders.

Some would be quick to blame Miss E.'s age. Maybe someone in her seventies didn't have the reflexes they did years ago, or maybe their eyesight wasn't as sharp. But I'd gripped the sides of my seat so hard my knuckles hurt while she effortlessly made that landing in the duster. I had no reason to doubt her reflexes or her eyesight.

It could have been the truck. It may have looked like it was in decent shape, but it was still thirty years old. It was at home on a county road, or hauling stuff around a farm, but it simply wasn't designed to be rolling down the highway surrounded by traffic.

Maybe it was the fact that when Miss E. started driving there wasn't a whole lot of traffic on the roads. Forget the traffic, there weren't a lot of roads. So maybe she just wasn't used to driving with so many other cars around.

But mostly I think Miss E.'s approach to driving came from her learning how to fly before learning how to drive. She was used to the open sky, the countryside or maybe an ocean spread out below her. She just didn't seem to notice the lines on the road or the signs beside it, or if she did, she didn't let them influence her driving. And the cars behind and beside her? Well, she changed lanes like the highway was a stretch of sky without a cloud in it. With the wind pouring through the windows and the hum of the knobby farm tires, the occasional horn blast went unnoticed.

As we got closer to San Francisco, we crested a hill, and I could see that the city was fogged in. The tops of buildings poked out of the clouds, seeming to float on nothingness, and the farthest tower of the Golden Gate Bridge was just a dim shadow in the white.

Rolling onto the bridge, we entered the fog. I could see the road ahead of us, at least a few cars ahead. And I could see the cables supporting the bridge, but their bright red was dulled to a grey. Everything else was fog – above, below us, on either side. Fog.

I think the feeling of flying must have struck us both at the same time, because when I turned to Miss E. she nodded before I said anything and her voice smiled. "Nice, isn't it, Bets?"

"Yeah," I said back, a little shaky. I don't know why I was nervous, but I was a little. I just couldn't get over the feeling that we were flying thousands of feet above the ground in Miss E.'s red pickup truck. I looked over at Miss E. again and thought about the day we sat in the Electra. Her right foot was on the gas pedal and her left hovered near the clutch, but they could have just as easily been on the rudder pedals. Her hands rested easily on a steering wheel that could have been an airplane yoke.

There was no sense fighting it. Instead, I rested my head back and enjoyed the view. It was a welcome relief after our drive on the highway, and before long I'd forgotten about the cars that could just barely be seen. When the fog started to thin ahead of us, I half expected to see the pointed tops of buildings emerge as we flew by them, but instead we saw their bottoms, rooted to the ground and edged in sidewalks and street lights. River and fog behind us, we'd made it to San Francisco.

The red pickup truck seemed slightly more comfortable on the city streets than on the highway, but Miss E.'s approach to driving didn't change at all. She still changed lanes whenever the urge struck her, and through a mix of weaving between other cars and scaring pedestrians back into doorways, she managed to keep a consistent speed while other drivers stayed mired in traffic all around her.

"Set the throttle, maintain a heading and altitude," she announced from the driver's seat. I wasn't sure if she was giving direction or simply encouraging herself, but I considered this unquestionable proof of my theory. Miss E. was simply better off in the air, so she drove like she was. And the farther I rode with her through the city streets, the more comfortable I became with her driving. It started to feel less like she was a bad driver and more and more like the roads had been built the wrong way, too straight, and not quite pointing in the right direction.

"Where we headed, Bets?" Miss E. asked as she swung the wheel around, making a left turn from the far right lane.

"Uh, Page Street. Fourteen Sixty-one." I hadn't thought to bring a map, but just saying the address made it feel like we were close, and for the first time since we'd left my front yard, the foolishness of what we were doing began to sink in. Emmie Hatcher didn't know me. She was unconscious before she landed in my lap, and she certainly wouldn't remember me holding her, wouldn't know I had her things or expect me to return them. I had her address. I could have just slipped her journal into an envelope or stuffed it along with her bag into a cardboard box and mailed them. It would have cost me a week's worth of delivering groceries, but Emmie would have gotten her stuff, and I wouldn't even have had to put a return address on it.

"We should go," I blurted. "We should go back home." Miss E. didn't respond, but a half block down the street she pulled into a space that looked too small and came to a stop with one wheel up on the curb. She just turned and looked at me as if she just shot down my idea and was waiting to hear if I had anything better. "We should go back home," I repeated. "This is dumb. Emmie doesn't need to see me or know who I am. Let's just mail this stuff, or leave it on the step or something. I didn't even do anything really. It's not like I saved her, just soaked up some of her blood with my T-shirt. I could have stepped in front of her I guess. I should have, but I just stood there watching. Then I took her stuff. I don't even know why I did it. I should have given it to one of the guys who helped her. Or followed after her. Or given it to someone. I just took it. I took it. I don't know why. And now I've had it. I've had it for weeks. And she's going to think, it's like, it's like I stole it, and..."

Miss E. cut me off with a silent raised hand.

For the first time on the whole drive, I think, she checked her side mirror and pulled back out into the street. We drove another block before she spoke.

"We're not here to return her stuff, Bets, and you know it. Postman comes to town all week, so that would have been the easiest way if that's all we needed to do. Why'd you come down here with me today, Bets?"

I sat stunned, trying to figure out how her sermon had suddenly turned into a pop quiz, and I had to let Miss E. take a few more seemingly random turns while I let her question and my answer churn in my head. What kept popping up while I searched for my next words was that her question made it sound like she was coming here anyway and just brought me along for the ride.

"I... I came down here to see Emmie Hatcher."

"To return her stuff?"

"No. Yes, but... no." Another block and another turn and then a flood of words.

"I wanted to see her, to meet her. I wanted to talk to her, because...because her father died in Vietnam. I wanted to talk to her, to ask her why she went to the protest that day, because I think her protesting the war is like her way of wishing her father back, and I wanted to ask her what I could do, if what I was doing was right, or enough, because I've been thinking that if I could do enough, if I could protest enough, like Emmie, that maybe the war would end. Maybe the war would end before my father gets killed."

The last sentence slipped from my mouth, and I became aware of all of my senses. It was like I'd forgotten them while I was talking and then suddenly remembered everything they were telling me once the words had gotten out. The smell of the truck, the seat below me and the sweat on the backs of my legs, the sound of the pickup's engine mixed with traffic, the too bright sunlight, and the sudden metallic taste in my mouth.

My hand was pulling on the door handle and struggling to push it open before I knew what I was doing. Miss E. must have seen my face go pale or seen it in my eyes, because she pulled to the side of the street with a sudden jerk of the wheel and a foot on the brake that helped throw open the door even as I fumbled with the handle.

I went from sitting to standing to hands and knees in one movement that was half running and half falling, and it felt like all the words I'd been keeping inside for months poured out of me in an endless bitter flow. I went from being aware of all my senses back to being aware of none, and only knew the horrible clenching that started in my stomach and pushed its way up and into my mouth.

Then it was over. I felt the street gravel on my hands, heard beeping car horns, and saw the mess that had just come out of me. I rolled to one side and ended up with my back against the bumper of a parked car, sweaty all over, cold and hot at the same time. I leaned my head back, closed my eyes, and realized that I was breathing again, feeling like I hadn't in hours. When I opened my eyes, Miss E. was crouched beside me. She pushed the hair out of my face and put a cloth to my head that felt impossibly cool. I sat up a little and she offered me a drink from the thermos cup she held in her hand. I half expected tomato juice, but instead it was cold water.

There were no questions. No wisdom-filled talk or knowing nods. Miss E. just crouched next to me, holding the cup and handing it back to me when I wanted more. When it seemed like I was ready to get up, she stood up first and offered me her hand. I teetered on unsteady feet, and Miss E. moved closer, slipping my arm over her shoulder. The red pickup was parked at a haphazard angle with a back corner stuck most of the way out into traffic. The cars stuck behind it and trying to merge into the other lane to get by were treated to the sight of a seventy-year-old woman helping a fifteen-year-old girl to climb back into an antique pickup truck.

Miss E. must have figured that my sudden exit from the pickup to get sick all over the streets of San Francisco was sign enough that I'd figured things out for myself and didn't need her to weigh in any longer. We rode in silence for the next few blocks and she made turns again like she'd lived in the city all her life. I was grateful for the absence of conversation and just rested my head back against the seat to let my thoughts wander. And what came to mind had nothing to do with Emmie, my father, or Vietnam. Instead I thought about the city I was in, the people I'd hoped to see the last time I was there, and the possibility of running into one of them while I was busting out of the red pickup truck helplessly throwing up. The thought made me queasy all over again.

There weren't any parking spaces in front of 1461 Page Street, and for the first time on our trip, Miss E. showed some awareness for the other cars around her and chose not to block traffic by simply making her own space. She let me climb out and drove off to look for a place to park. I wondered again about my mother letting me go for a drive with someone she'd just met, and then wondered at Miss E. dropping off a teenager on a city street so I could go knock on the door of a house whose occupant I'd only met while she was unconscious and bleeding to death. I'd pretty much figured Miss E. out by then though, and knew that she was deliberate in everything. This was one conversation she knew she wasn't part of.

Emmie Hatcher's house looked like so many others we'd passed on our way through the city. It was in an older section of San Francisco where the houses had stood long enough to get a comfortable shabbiness around the edges, only partly hidden by the half-hearted effort of their owners to spruce them up with a fresh coat of paint and some flowers out front. A clear sign of who lived there, the brick stairway of Emmie's house led to a doorway adorned with a peace sign, and in the open upstairs windows tie dyed sheets repurposed as curtains drifted lazily.

I climbed the steps quickly and knocked on the door. I'd left any hesitation I'd had on the street a few blocks back. The first floor windows were open as well, and music from some room farther back in the house had found its way out onto the porch along with a smoky smell that was like a mixture of incense, candles, and campfire.

I'm pretty sure that by Mr. Johnson's definition, or anyone else's, the guy who answered the door was a hippie. His hair was longer than mine, and the stubble on his chin was halfway between an attempt at a beard and shaving neglect. His shirt was open in front and hung down below his waist, where torn blue jeans flared toward falling-apart sandals. The smell and the music emerged from the house with him, and his eyes seemed to take in the whole street and float toward the sky before they focused on the source of the knocking.

I asked for Emmie and watched him think for a moment, like his mind was wandering back through the rooms of the house and up stairways in search of someone belonging to that name. I saw the connection click into place, and he nodded.

"Yeah. Yeah, Emmie lives here."

I waited for a few seconds and then prompted, "Could I see her?"

He didn't reply, but thought for a few seconds before turning his head back into the house. "Hey, Emmie! Someone here to see you!" he shouted, then added in a quieter voice, almost to himself as he walked away from me, "It's a kid..."

I bristled a little at the word. Emmie seemed like she was college age, whether or not she was going to school, and I'd figured that she lived in some sort of group house if she wasn't living with family. So I was expecting to meet some college students, or at least some people who could be college students. But I guess I'd wrestled long enough with what happened at City Hall to think of myself as older than the average high school freshman, if not in years, at least in experience. I felt more of a connection to the protesters who had stormed through the doors that day than the high school students in the pep rally where I'd caused such a stir. Part of me wanted to be welcomed into the house on Page Street as an equal, definitely not as a kid who'd stopped by to see if Emmie could come out and play.

I was left standing on the porch in front of the open door not knowing if I should enter or not. Emmie's housemate had long since disappeared into the depths of the house, and Emmie hadn't come to greet me yet. I shifted from one foot to another until I felt too uncomfortable waiting, and then stepped through the doorway.

The music and the smoky smell of the house were stronger as soon as I entered. It felt rude to walk in and leave the door wide open, so I closed it behind me and instantly felt like I'd cut off the outside world. There was a room with couches and chairs off the entryway to my right and a few people sitting there looked up at the sound of the closing door. I saw the hippie who'd answered my knock, already seated and blending in with his housemates. Another looked from me to the stairway and back again, and then one called again for Emmie.

"Coming," came a distant voice from up the stairway. I let out a sigh of relief that puffed my cheeks. A nagging thought had started in the back of my mind that this was not even Emmie's house and the guy who had greeted me at the door was too out of it to even know who he was sharing a house with. Knowing that I was actually in Emmie Hatcher's house put me back on the right track.

Emmie showed up a minute later, drifting down the stairs in a flowing wisp of hair and flowery dress. Seeing her gave me a rush of memory, and the images flashed with each step she took down the stairs. Emmie running – step. Emmie spinning out of control – step. Emmie hitting the wall – step.

She moved quickly at first, like she was coming down the stairs to meet someone she was expecting, but her feet stuttered when she saw me and had no idea who I was.

"Hi," she said with question and hesitation in her voice, and her foot pausing halfway between steps.

"Hi," I answered with equal hesitation. It would have been so much easier if she remembered me from the protest, or showed at least some glimmer of recognition. "I, uhh... I have your diary. Your diary from that day... that day at City Hall." There were a million things I wanted to tell her, to ask her, but that was the best I could do.

I could see that the foot farthest down the stairway took a slight step backward, like retreating up the stairway would let her pull back from the memory I'd brought her. "My diary? From City Hall?" was her only answer as her eyes sifted through the information they'd been given. I held up her bag and then reached in to pull out the diary, offering it to her with a lopsided shrug.

Realization came to her with a sharp intake of breath and eyes clenched closed. When her eyes opened again, they seemed to be looking through me and back toward the memory of City Hall. "You were there. That day?" There was question and answer in her voice, and I wasn't sure if I needed to give an explanation or simply nod in affirmation.

I did both with a shudder in my own voice. "Yeah," I whispered, knowing it would be enough. Emmie took the last few steps to the landing and then held the railing as she took the remaining two to the floor. I held out her bag and diary and her eyes jumped from one to the other before taking them slowly.

"Thanks."

The exchange could have been over at that point. Emmie could have turned and gone back upstairs or opened the front door for me to leave, but she didn't. She just stood in front of me. I waited for more, but since she'd spoken last, it seemed like the next move was mine.

"I thought maybe I could talk with you." Emmie's eyes squinted a little, looking at me, and I saw them flicker toward the front door and beyond as if she were teetering on the edge of just getting rid of me. "About that day," I added. "And some other stuff."

As if understanding that the events in City Hall were as significant for me as they were for her, even if she didn't know why, Emmie nodded then glanced toward the room full of long haired look-alikes and tilted her head toward the second floor. "Yeah, we should talk," she said and turned to climb the stairs. I followed her up creaking and worn steps. The house's facelift had only gone as far as the outside. We reached a long hallway where I could see through doorways into multiple rooms. Emmie made a U-turn at the top of the stairs and walked down the hallway back toward the front of the house. She disappeared through a doorway and I followed.

Not having seen the rest of the house, it was hard to know, but Emmie's room had to be the best. The front wall held two arch-topped windows that looked out on the street below and the skyline beyond. I hadn't been paying enough attention on the drive in, but it was clear from the view that Page Street sat atop a hill that provided a view of the neighborhood below and a glimpse of the fog that surely hung over the bay and Golden Gate Bridge. Emmie's room was one that I saw from the street, and the tie-dyed curtains billowed toward me and then settled back in a welcoming come-here gesture. Emmie took the same approach and plunked herself down in a chair and then gestured toward an unclear resting place for me, either bed, window seat, or floor. I opted for the window and tucked my knees up under my chin to fit myself into the narrow but comfortable space.

Since I had come out of nowhere with Emmie's belongings, and since I probably had a more complete memory of what had happened that day, I figured I should go first and fill in the gaps. I told Emmie about the field trip and why I was in San Francisco. I told her about Mr. Flynn's plan to expose us to the anti-war sentiment and about how it had trapped us in the middle of everything. I saw Emmie mouth the word "cool" and nod at the first part and then mouth "oh shit" at the second. I could have skipped over the crushing feeling outside the doors and the panic I'd felt, but I didn't, mostly because I felt like I deserved more than observer status. I saw Emmie shift uncomfortably when I got to the part where her story and mine met. Although she had more room on the chair than I did on the window seat, Emmie pulled her knees to her chin like me and seemed to hide behind them. Realizing I didn't need to give any more details to a chapter that clearly made Emmie uncomfortable,

I moved on to my story back at school and wrapped up with the pep rally and my shirt. I didn't mention my father.

I saw Emmie mouth the word "cool" again with that affirming nod and then say it out loud. "Cool. Yeah... cool," she said a second time for emphasis, or maybe because she didn't know what else to say.

There was a long enough silence that I started to wonder if that was it. I'd returned her stuff and given her an explanation of how I'd gotten them and why I'd kept them longer than I probably should. I thought Emmie would eventually stand up and thank me and then usher me toward back downstairs and out the door. But she was just letting it sink in, making the connections between her protest at City Hall and mine at school, her situation and mine.

"Your father is in the war?" she said, finally breaking the silence. I nodded, and there was silence again while that sank in, but it eventually made all the pieces fit together. Then she told me her story. Some of it I knew, some of it I'd guessed.

"My father went to Vietnam last year," she began. "We got one letter from him telling us that he was there and that he was OK and settling in. Then we didn't hear from him. We waited, figuring he wasn't able to write or that the mail was just slow." I must have nodded or something, or Emmie just figured I knew what she was talking about.

"You know what it's like, huh? They send two soldiers to your house. Did you know that? When they tell you, they don't want someone to do that alone I guess, so they send two." I didn't actually know that, but nodded like I did. My mind was already racing, imagining what it would be like to see an unfamiliar car pull up in front of my house and watch two soldiers step out.

"My father lasted two weeks in Vietnam before he was killed. Just his luck, I guess. The soldiers gave us details about what had happened but I don't remember much of it. They were trying to take some hill. A hill. Who would fight over a hill?" Emmie's frustration pushed her out of her chair and over to the other window, where she stood a long time, just looking out and leaning against the window frame.

"This is a bad war," she finally sighed. "We keep sending people, and they keep getting killed, and it seems like no one can really tell us why we're even over there. Or at least they can't give us a reason that sounds like it's worth fathers and sons dying.

"Lots of people protest the war because it's cool not to like the war. And some people go to protests because they think it's going to be a party." Emmie laughed a nervous laugh and shook her head a little, "There's a room full of them downstairs.

"This is a bad war," Emmie said again. "I went to City Hall that day because I wanted people to know that." Pretty eyes that should have been smiling at boys looked up at the ceiling to hold back tears.

"You feel helpless, you know? Like all this is just happening around you and you can't do anything. But not doing anything is like saying it's alright. And there's a whole bunch of people not doing anything. So I'm the unlucky one

I guess. I got bounced around by the police and ended up in the hospital, but it doesn't change anything. This war is still just shit." Emmie had turned away from the window to face me, her hands balled into fists.

"You were right about why I was at the rally. Maybe I didn't even realize it at the time, but I wanted to do something to fix what happened to my father. I don't mean bring him back. I'm not crazy or anything. But in a way it will fix things sort of, if it means someone else's dad isn't going to die fighting this dumb war." There was another long silence while Emmie flipped through her diary. I'd read enough of it to guess at which pages she lingered on.

"You're doing the right thing, Elizabeth," she said, closing the diary. It felt right to hear Emmie say my name like that. Bets would always be my father's name for me, but it was a little girl's name. The way Emmie said my name, Elizabeth, sounded grown up. "The t-shirt at the pep rally, that was cool. If you're shaking people up, you must be doing something right. Keep shaking." She nodded slowly and left her last sentence hang in the room for a while and it felt alright for both of us to just sit there, not saying anything and just thinking. I'm not sure what Emmie was thinking about, but I was thinking about shaking people up.

We sat in her room a while longer, but our conversation about City Hall, bloody t-shirts, and Vietnam was over. Emmie flipped through her diary again and shared some entries about moving out of her home and starting college, and an entry about a boy she met. Maybe that was who she'd expected at the bottom of the stairs. I told her about moving last summer and settling into school and my job delivering groceries. Emmie nodded and smiled like she knew exactly what I was talking about when I told her about the freedom of riding my bike. She fell on the floor and practically peed her pants when I told her about how I knocked out Peter Anderson.

Being with Emmie felt right. I had Cassie and other friends at school, but sitting in Emmie's room that afternoon was different. We talked and told stories that we knew the other would understand completely. Some we laughed at, some made us cry a little. Either way, it felt like we were doing it together. Maybe it was because of our fathers, maybe because of what had happened at City Hall, but for the first time since my father left, I felt like I was talking to someone who understood me completely. So what I said next completely surprised me and felt absolutely right.

"I came here today with Amelia Earhart." Emmie half giggled but saw my face and knew right away it wasn't some joke that she just didn't understand. So instead of laughing, she stopped and sat quietly looking at me, waiting for me to say more. I told her about the grocery deliveries. I told her about the Electra and the duster. I didn't tell her everything. There were details that were really just part of Miss E.'s story, and I didn't think it was fair to tell. If Emmie had asked about Amelia's reasons for doing what she did, I would have dodged the question. But she didn't. She just listened to everything I had to say then nodded and smiled when I finished, giving me what must be her standard response to anything she truly feels good about.

"Cool. Yeah, that's cool."

It was time to go. I felt like it was. We'd said everything we needed to say and then made everything right by spending another hour talking about whatever else we wanted to tell each other. Me sharing about Miss E. sealed it. It was my biggest secret and there was nothing that Emmie could share to top it. After months of telling no one, it felt good to finally talk to someone about Miss E.

We stood up at the same time, and I found my way back to the stairs with Emmie trailing behind. I could have stopped and turned at the front door to say my goodbyes, but I didn't. I walked straight out and Emmie followed. I knew why.

Miss E. had somehow found a parking space right in front of the house, and she stood waiting for me, leaning comfortably on the front fender of the red pickup. I looked over my shoulder to make sure Emmie was there and smiled when I saw that she was. We bounced down the front steps together and then stood side by side in front of Miss E.

"Well, Bets, you have everything sorted out? Looks like it."

"Yeah, it was good," I said with a smile and a nod. "This is Emmie. Emmie Hatcher." It was a one-sided introduction and Miss E. knew it.

Emmie stretched out her hand. "It's an honor to meet you, Ma'am," she said with a smile.

"No need for Ma'am," Miss E. responded, taking Emmie's hand in hers. "Amelia will do just fine."

"Well then, it's an honor to meet you Amelia," Emmie smiled.

"Likewise," Miss E. smiled back. "I hear you're quite the activist." Emmie just shrugged, but her eyes sparkled with excitement and pride. "Thanks for visiting with Bets. Seems like you helped her do some important thinking."

"She's cool... yeah, she's cool." Emmie extended her hand and shook Miss E.'s and then turned to me and gave me a hug. Then she bounced back up the steps to her door and gave a quick wave before disappearing inside.

Landing

I wasn't really paying attention as we left Emmie's house and Miss E. wound her way back through the streets of San Francisco. I was thinking about the things Emmie had said, and thinking about what I could do when I got back to Forestville. It wasn't until we were crossing the bridge that I realized it was a different bridge and that Miss E. was taking a different route out of the city.

"How do you know where you're going?"

Miss E. shrugged. "One road leads to another," she said in a way that just made it sound like fact. If anyone else had said it, the phrase would have come out sounding like some mystical proverb or half-joking bumper sticker. Miss E. just said it like that was the way things worked, and I knew it was all the answer I was going to get.

The bridge turned into a highway once we crossed it, but instead of stepping on the gas and picking up speed, Miss E. changed lanes and took the first exit.

I waited a few minutes in silence before asking, "Are we going somewhere?"

"Yes we are. You didn't think I drove all the way down here just so you could visit your friend, did you?"

I did, in fact, think that. So I tried to hide my confusion while I sorted through the reasons Miss E. might have for coming to San Francisco. The roar of a plane overhead interrupted my thoughts, and then the red pickup bumped onto an unpaved side road before coming to a halt with its nose toward the water. Another plane tore through the air above as Miss E. climbed out of the truck. This time, I was able to watch it continue on its path until it landed just across a shipping channel from where we'd parked. An airport.

Miss E. was already hopping up onto the hood of the pickup when I got out, and she patted a spot next to her, inviting me up. I had a memory of my father doing the same thing, but I pushed it to the back of my mind and joined Miss E. on the hood.

The view wasn't especially pleasant. To our left, docks and cranes lined the channel on either side and ships choked the docks. To our right, a spit of land that looked like it had been entirely paved over stuck out into the bay and seemed to hold nothing but trucks and shipping containers. San Francisco rose in the distance separated from us by the choppy gray bay, too far away to even feel a part of our scenery. But ahead of us and much closer, lay the low flat runaways of Oakland Airport.

Miss E. lay back on the hood of the pickup with her head resting on the windshield, and I did the same. The only view was the sky above us, so I just took it all in. Sunny blue, clouds drifting by. I waited, wondering if Miss E. had brought me here for another talk, but hoped that she hadn't, that she just wanted to relax and let the clouds blowing by clear our thoughts.

Then, the plane roared by.

The sound came without me noticing at first, gradually getting closer and louder, but slowly enough that I didn't notice it was even there until it was so loud it filled the air completely. The sky vanished and all that was left was plane, the underside of the wings, the landing gear, the sound.

I slid back on the hood so I could sit with my back up against the windshield, watching as the plane crossed the channel, getting lower and lower, and then finally touching down. There was a sound that was maybe half real, but far enough away that it was maybe half imagined too, just to punctuate the change from wings in the air to wheels on the ground.

Landing – I'd only done it twice. The first time there was so much happening at once and I was so panicked, I was just glad to be safely on the ground. The second time, I had a chance to enjoy it, and I was left with the surprising feeling of how slowly we approached the ground, how it gradually got closer, and then in a breath we were rolling across it. On the ground so quickly, it made me wonder that we had ever been in the air at all.

And then I realized where we were.

"This is where you took off from." Miss E.'s silence answered my question. "And this is where you were going to land." There was more silence from Miss E., but I wasn't expecting an answer. Miss E. wasn't going to waste words telling me something I already knew.

It was like looking through the wrong end of a telescope. Instead of seeing the airport close up, it looked like it was far, far away. I saw it like I was sitting in the Electra, looking out across that beautiful flat field Miss E. had described. I realized we were on the other end of that perfect take off and that short easy flight that Miss E. had been dreaming about for the last thirty years.

"I haven't been here in a long time, Bets." Miss E. finally spoke. "You watched me start up my plane and came up on me while I was closing the barn door on it, and you probably figured I sit out there in that cockpit more than keeping the engines in good condition requires. Old ladies are allowed their eccentricities.

"But I haven't been here in a long, long time," she repeated and I wasn't sure if she was telling me or telling herself. "I couldn't. I knew seeing this place would make me want to fly here, and I couldn't do that." She paused and then corrected herself. "I wasn't ready to do that."

The sound of another plane grew behind us, and then filled the air overhead. The place was perfect for the way Miss E. had a conversation. Enough time between planes to get out what needed to be said, followed by forced silence while the plane landed. Time to think and no time for me to ask questions.

"Bets, I've got to hand it to you, you're the bee's knees when it comes to shaking things up, but I think I knew that right from the start." She could have just been talking about the pep rally, but I knew it was something else too. "There's lots of people in town that needed shaking up, Bets, myself included."

Another plane.

"Not sure how this will all end, Bets. I'm pretty sure you'll figure things out for yourself and do what you decide needs to be done. You certainly don't need an old lady telling you how to manage things. And you should probably start spending more time paying attention to the boys at school and less time sitting at my kitchen table."

I grimaced a little, definitely not ready for a conversation with Miss E. about boys. Another plane overhead saved my life, and cut off any protest over Miss E.'s claim that I spent too much time in her kitchen.

"I landed in a lot of places, and I met a lot of people while I was flying all over, Bets. Landing was always the best part. Lots of folks excited to say hello. Getting to the next place, and then the next place, just comes with being a flyer. But part of me never liked leaving where I was, never liked saying goodbye. Too many people to say goodbye to most of the time, and sometimes saying goodbye to a person was just too hard. Lots of times, I would tip my wings a bit once I was in the air and hope folks understood that it was the best I could do."

While her words were falling into place in my mind, another plane landed. Before it had touched down on the runway, Miss E. slid off the hood and climbed into the pick-up. I followed. I'd learned enough about Miss E. to know she was done talking.

Protest Revisited

I t took a few days of planning.

The pep rally had been on a Thursday, and since my mother had let me take the following day off, I'd had a three-day weekend, but everyone at school had a day to spread the story and talk about what it all meant. I had the spotlight all to myself when I showed up at school Monday morning. I intended to take advantage of it.

At first, all anyone wanted to talk to me about was all the disruption I'd caused, how there was no control in classrooms after the pep rally, and how none of the teachers were really able to teach anything on Friday either. I got my share of high-fives and pats on the back. But after that died down, the students who'd done a little more thinking found their way over to me. They were subtle, someone opening a locker next to mine, another behind me in the lunch line, someone else keeping pace with me in the hallways long enough for a conversation. And while the first group just wanted to relive the excitement of the previous week and tell me their piece of a story I already knew, the second group had questions. They'd already figured out the "why", and after talking to me they left knowing what was next.

I talked to twenty-three people that day. I mean twenty-three that I really talked to, not the ones who just wanted to know if I could do something else crazy to get them out of class. I wrote their names on an inside page of my notebook. I asked each of them to talk to five friends, and to tell their friends to do the same. I was still struggling to keep an A in first period math, but even I could figure out that a couple multiplication problems equaled half the school ready to go along with my plan.

With that many people involved, I knew everything had to be done just right. I thought back to the waves of people outside City Hall. They all wanted the same thing, all wanted to be heard, all wanted an end to the war. But the hippie with the megaphone got it wrong. I wouldn't make the same mistake.

I checked back with my original twenty-three on Wednesday. Each name in my notebook got a little star next to it and a number, the number of students they'd recruited. Not everyone had reached out to a full five times five, and some contact lists included some overlap. We still had a lot of names. I went over the plan again with each of them, and gave them a list of what not to do. They would spread the word again and then talk to me again on Thursday to confirm that the message had gotten out.

On Friday morning, I was at school early and had already dropped off my things in my locker and grabbed my books before most of the students even arrived. I tried to stand back and watch things like a teacher or like Mr. Higgins, wondering if anything looked out of place. Maybe some kids were dressed a little differently. Maybe there were more kids bringing lunches than there normally would be, especially on a Friday pizza day. But other than that, I thought things looked like any other day. I tried to identify kids who were involved in my plan. Other than the twenty-three I'd talked to, I didn't really know who else had been recruited, just how many. No one stood out. Nothing would look wrong to someone who didn't know what to look for. I ducked into my first period class before the bell rang.

Lunch was different. Someone scanning the cafeteria would have noticed the changes right away. The funny thing was there were several people doing just that, scanning the cafeteria, making sure everyone stayed in their seat, didn't get too noisy, and didn't throw food. But their senses had been so dulled by the day-in, day-out buzz of cafeteria noise that they didn't notice anything. They didn't notice that a lot of kids who brought a brown paper bag or a thermos were standing in line to buy lunch anyway. They didn't notice that the usual rainbow of t-shirts was a little bit lighter, a little bit whiter that day. And they didn't notice that instead of eating, most kids were just looking at each other or the clock on the wall.

There was nothing special about 12:16. It was just a time I'd picked. If anyone was paying attention at 12:15, they would have noticed a whole cafeteria of high school kids taking the lids off the thermoses they'd borrowed from younger siblings, dug out of the backs to cupboards, or bought new the day before. High school kids just didn't bring thermoses to school. But no one was paying attention. I was counting on that. And then at 12:16, we did it.

We all stood up. We grabbed our thermoses and poured tomato juice down the fronts of our white t-shirts. In an instant, the room went from sitting to standing, from white to red, and amazingly, from noisy to silent. We all just stood there in silence

The three people in charge didn't know what to do, so they stood there too. A few ladies from the kitchen popped their heads out the door when the cafeteria went silent, but they retreated back into the kitchen as quickly as they came. Some kids who weren't in on the plan figured things out and decided to improvise with shared tomato juice or ketchup packets.

Then we grabbed our things and walked out. There was no pushing or shoving. There was no shouting. No one needed a megaphone to tell us what to do or to get our message across. We could have walked across the main hallway and right out the main doors, but we took a longer path that led us by classrooms, through the gym, and finally past the main office. We picked up more along the way, some kids who were already out in the hallways, but more who were in classrooms and decided to get up and leave.

Mr. Higgins was standing outside the main office when we walked by. His eyes stared at me behind the flashing lenses of his glasses, but there was nothing he could do. He certainly couldn't put all of us in the office and call our mothers. If he did, some of them probably would have joined us. He raised a hand as if trying stop our progress, but then slowly put it down and just watched open mouthed.

We made our way back toward the cafeteria and then out the main doors and down the steps. El Molino High School was set back from the road, and patches of grass and trees and benches isolated it from Front Street. The shade of the trees and a place to sit were inviting, but we passed them by and instead lined the sidewalk on Front Street. There were a lot of us. Some kids had skipped out of an art class and had enough foresight to bring a container of red paint. Students who didn't have the nerve to leave in the middle of class, walked out of school during a change of classes, and kids who hadn't seen our parade through the main building were drawn in as they cut across school grounds to their next class.

In a brief moment of panic, I was reminded of the people on the edge of the crowd in San Francisco, those drawn in by the noise who ended up fueling the fire. I thought how quickly someone who hadn't been in on the original plan could easily turn things for the worse with an angry shout, but I looked left and right down the sidewalks of Front Street and I knew this was a different sort of protest. There were smiles and there was some singing. Without realizing I was doing it, I reached out for the hands of the people on either side of me, and then watched as the hand holding moved in a chain reaction from one person to the next, and then the next.

Cars on Front Street honked horns. Most people rolled down windows and waved or flashed peace signs. Every once in a while someone drove by and shouted, but their anger was drowned out by singing. Lots of kids had brought along notebooks like I had to the pep rally. Signs were made and passed along down the sidewalk. If someone in town hadn't heard about my blood covered shirt and protest at the pep rally, they certainly knew what we were about once they saw our sidewalk filled with "No War", "Peace", and "Soldiers Come Home" signs.

Eventually, a police car pulled up. Again, I had visions of City Hall, but when the policeman emerged from his car, rather than confronting our line of red stained t-shirts, he walked across the street and had a short conversation with a menacing group who'd been gathering there. Shoulders were shrugged and shoes scuffed stones into the road before the group climbed back in their cars and drifted away.

The police car stayed parked on the side of the street the rest of the time we were in front of the school. I saw the policeman walk up and down the sidewalk a few times and stop to talk to a few kids here and there. Later in the day, during what passed for rush hour in Forestville, he stood in the middle of the street directing the cars to keep moving when they slowed to see what was going on. Even with his help, traffic was backed up for blocks, and I'm pretty sure I saw some cars drive by more than once, like they'd circled around for another pass to get a better look.

It must have been a slow news day in Santa Rosa. Crawling along with the rush hour cars, was a news van from the *Santa Rosa Star*. Forestville didn't have a newspaper of its own, so the local news was reported in the *Star*, but other than high school sports and the annual church bazaar, Forestville didn't generate much news. I watched the van roll slowly down the street and turn down a side street where it could park.

What few parking spaces there were on Front Street were now taken up by the ever expanding line of protesters who had spilled from the sidewalk, onto the curb, and into the street. We'd become more than just students from the high school. People were hopping out of cars to come talk to us, and most were staying. Customers coming out of Johnson's store or the post office were wandering down to see what the commotion was. Notebook signs and a fresh supply of tomato juice from Johnson's were distributed.

The sidewalk in front of school could no longer hold us, and people were on both sides of the street. Adults were mixed in with students by then, but when Mr. Flynn took his place on the curb I immediately noticed him. My first reaction was to run to him, and I took a step off the curb ready to dodge through the line of traffic to the other side of the street. But I didn't have to. Mr. Flynn's smile and his peace sign raised high over his head was enough. I returned his smile, made a gesture that was half peace sign and half excited wave, and then returned my attention to the protest, holding my notebook sign and joining in the cheers.

It took a half hour for the newspaper reporter to make his way back to the front of the school. The closest parking space was apparently not that close at all. I could see him farther down Front Street stopping every so often to talk to someone. Some shrugged their shoulders or shook their heads, but most nodded and pointed my way. When he got close enough, I heard him call my name. I tried to step toward the back of the line but I felt hands pushing me forward and out into the street. I found out later that the reporter had started out trying to ask some questions to the first people he'd come to, but they either didn't feel like they had any answers or told him to talk to me. As he worked his way down the line he got snippets of the story, heard about the pep rally and about my organizing earlier that week, and had decided for himself that I was the one he needed to talk to if he wanted the whole story.

I gave him the best answers I could. I told him my version of San Francisco, the t-shirt, and the pep rally. I told him about my father and how he was in Vietnam, but I was careful to make sure he understood that the story was not one girl wanting her father to come home from the war. Maybe that was still all I wanted last week, but somewhere between the pep rally, my visit to Emmie's, and my talk with Miss E. at the airport, I had realized anything I did needed to be about more. So the story the reporter left with was about a high school and a town that had decided they were ready for the war to end.

I was glad I was only talking to a newspaper reporter rather than someone with a television camera. I knew that whatever he wrote about me, no one would end up hearing my stammered answers or seeing my blushed responses. I was pretty focused on my answers while I was talking to him. I wanted to get it right, so for the five or ten minutes that I talked with him, the protest stretching down the street faded into the background. As we wrapped things up though, my eyes looked over the reporter's shoulder to the still slow traffic on Front Street where I saw the red pickup truck roll by.

Arrivals and Departures

I would have been fooling myself if I thought that the protest I had organized did much to change the course of the war. The world is a big, big place, and Forestville is pretty small, even with some help from the *Santa Rosa Star*.

In Forestville, we had the weekend to talk about what we'd done. It was no coincidence that our line of protesters in front of the high school was not too far down Front Street from the town hall. The mayor wanted in on the action and stood in the town square Saturday afternoon to give his support to our protest in a speech that was careful enough not to offend anyone in town who supported the war. Though the point had been made and most of the students originally involved stayed at home, there was still a small group of people lining the sidewalks most of the weekend.

The article about the protest appeared in the Sunday edition of the *Star*, and people around town all seemed pretty pleased with the way the protest was presented. I read and reread the article paying extra attention to the lines where I was quoted. I sat across the kitchen table from my mother as she read it out loud to me even though I'd already read it to myself twenty times. She had already gotten all the details from me, and I knew she approved of what I'd done, but hearing the pride in her voice and seeing her nod and smile as she read the newspaper that Sunday morning was still better than everything else combined.

About a week later, an envelope arrived for me in the mail with Emmie Hatcher's return address on it. I hadn't given her my address, but my name and Forestville, CA, was enough. The post office had done the rest. I tore it open to discover a newspaper clipping from the San Francisco Examiner. The paper ran local news stories in a mid-week section that covered the larger San Francisco area, and they'd picked up on the *Star's* story. It was a shortened version of the article, but it got all the important points and reached thousands of readers instead of hundreds, depending on how many people read the back page of the "Area News" section. I was a little surprised anyone in Emmie's house even read the paper, but the envelope contained only the newspaper clipping with Emmie's familiar handwriting at the bottom. "Cool. Very Cool! Keep Shaking!"

A week later another envelope came addressed to my mother. A letter from my father. There had been enough going on in my life that I wasn't checking the mailbox every afternoon waiting for a letter from him, but I was aware that it had been longer than normal since the last time he'd written. So my mother and I were at the kitchen table again, this time sitting on the same side, both clustered around the single page.

My eyes darted from line to line taking in my father's news, but my mother had gotten a head start and cried out, thrusting her hands into the air along with the letter before I got to the end. I jumped from my seat to grab the letter back, but my mother jumped up with me. Before I could take it from her, the letter was dropped to the table, and my mother's arms were around me.

"He's coming home."

It was my second trip to Oakland in one month. This time I sat beside my mother, and we drove right onto the base rather than watching it from a distance. My mother mostly drove in silence. I suppose we were both lost in our thoughts, excited about my father's return, but we'd both remained nervous and unwilling to fully share the excitement until he was back with us. Despite my mother's silence, her driving was loads better than Miss E.'s.

There were a lot of families there that day. A cargo plane outfitted as a troop carrier could hold a lot of soldiers, and there were a few planes scheduled to land in Oakland. The base wasn't really designed for a bunch of waiting wives and their kids. It was set up to move soldiers. The men stationed there did what they could to take care of us, but in the end we were just a crowd of people waiting on the tarmac for the next plane to land. All I could do was stand next to my mother and wait.

We watched as soldiers climbed down the stair of the first plane to land. Anyone who's ever waited in an airport to pick someone up, knows a little bit how I felt that day. You keep seeing people who look like the person you're waiting for. One after another, for a split second you start toward them, or your heart jumps, then you realize it's not them yet. Now put everyone in a uniform so they all look the same, and multiply the anticipation by one hundred. Then multiply it again. My father wasn't on the first plane.

The second plane landed about an hour later. All of the men coming off the airplane steps looked the same, until – there was no mistaking him, the way he walked, the way he looked around while coming down the steps, and the way he smiled.

We were waiting in a roped off area meant to keep us safe so the planes could taxi off the runway without getting too close and families could reunite without too much chaos. But there was no way the ropes could hold me back. I'd never tried out for the track team, but I guess I would have been a shoo-in for the hurdles. I cleared the rope barrier in one stride, only vaguely aware of the soldiers calling after me to wait.

The next thing I knew, my arms were wrapped around my father and his were wrapped around me. I held him forever, breathing in his scent, hearing his voice. I buried my face in his chest and covered his shirt with happy tears. I held him as tightly as I could, and then I held him tighter. He was home.

We walked arm in arm back to my mother, and then I gave him up briefly to let my mother have her turn. I watched the two of them, and understood better what my mother was feeling all the long time that he was gone. After I waited as long as I could, I interrupted their moment to hug them both together, pushing myself between them and squeezing them closer together at the same time. We broke apart long enough to look into each other's eyes and then hugged again.

We were walking away from the airfield, the three of us holding hands, when I heard the Electra. Even if I'd still been watching and waiting for planes, I would have heard it before I saw it, I think. After sitting in the cockpit between those two engines, there was no mistaking the sound they made.

I stopped in my tracks and pulled free from my parents' hands to turn and look for the plane. Everyone still on the tarmac was looking to the sky for the next plane to land, but this was different. There was a hush. Soldiers took off their hats to shield their eyes from the sun and scratched their heads. Wives, initially disappointed when they realized the plane wasn't a troop carrier, took children's hands and everyone refocused their attention on the sky. Families already walking away stopped and turned back. Soldiers emerged from hangars to search for the noisy plane, but my father was the first to spot it, and my eyes followed his arrow-straight arm to the dot growing larger in the sky.

In the barn, the Electra had seemed motionless and frozen. Watching it in the sky was like going to an art museum and suddenly seeing the paintings spring to life. Now it was speeding toward us, too large to be in the sky, and yet gracefully streaming through it, getting closer and bigger every second.

The Oakland base wasn't big enough to have a control tower, but I was sure that the radio building was full of soldiers scrambling for headphones and radar screens, frantically trying to figure out who or what was about to land on their runway. I remembered what Miss E. had told me about all the modern communications equipment that the Electra didn't have, and figured at some point the men would simply give up, toss their headphones aside, and just come outside to watch the plane with everyone else.

The Electra was treetop level now. I'd watched the big troop carriers lumbering down to the runway, and it was easy to see how much steadier the Electra was. After all, its pilot had flown around the world and back again. It was as if the Electra were suspended in the air and we were moving toward it, the Earth rotating beneath it and moving closer each second. The plane hung above the runway, and I held my breath waiting for the wheels to touch. They were above the runway, above it, above it, and then they were rolling on it. Just like that.

I heard the engines' sound change, saw the flaps and rudder adjust, and pictured Miss E. pulling levers and working pedals.

Once the plane landed, I could think only of its pilot. As she taxied closer, I squinted to see in the windows, to get a look at her. But I didn't really need to, I'd already seen her flying the Electra that day in the barn, and I knew she was smiling her Amelia Earhart smile.

The Electra paused on the tarmac only for a second, not even long enough for the people watching it to take a step toward it. The engines revved up again and the rudder and rear wheel turned hard to the left. The plane made a half circle turn, pointed back down the runway, and then its engines roared. There was a second delay, the time it took for the blurred propellers to cut through enough air to start moving the weight of the plane again, just enough time to wonder if the plane would take off at all. In that short second, I thought of all the runways, airports, and grassy fields Amelia had taken off from. I was lucky enough to be with her on two take offs, but the one I watched in Oakland would remain clearest in my memory.

The wheels were on the runway, and then magically they weren't. The Electra stuck to its course over the length of the runway, Amelia steering a straighter path through the air than she did on all the roads between Forestville and San Francisco. Then it banked slowly to the right as it climbed. All eyes on the ground watched it slowly circle the airfield until it was pointing back toward us. Necks bent skyward as the plane flew directly overhead, and then we watched as it grew smaller and smaller on a path that took it due west, and onward out over the ocean to whatever lay beyond.

I'm sure most people on the ground that day didn't even notice the Electra's wings tip back and forth as it disappeared toward the horizon. If they did, they probably thought it was a bit of rough air, or maybe the pilot adjusting for a new heading. I knew it was Amelia waving goodbye. I waved back. I waved back until I couldn't see the Electra any longer, and then I took my mother and father's hands and went home.

There are all kinds of theories about Amelia Earhart's last flight. People have searched for wreckage on the bottom of the ocean and found unexplained objects on tiny Pacific islands. Others think she was a spy, captured by the Japanese. Maybe one day they'll discover something out in the ocean that makes them think they've found the answer. I'll keep quiet and let them think what they want. I don't really know what became of Miss E. after she flew away from Oakland that day, I just know that her last flight was at least thirty years later than most people think it was.

Epilogue

The wind blows the tall grass as I walk up the low hill from my plane. Its powerful engines and electronic navigation made crossing the wide ocean and finding the tiny island feel almost like cheating, but it was challenging enough that the solid ground is welcoming beneath my feet.

The view from the top of the hill shows me the expanse of the surrounding ocean and the rugged airstrip below. My eyes trace the route I'd just followed from the west and then turn toward far away Hawaii and California beyond that. I've come a long way, and I'm almost home. Others have flown the same route and have recognized this place with a tip of their wings or a dropped wreath. I needed to do more. I needed to land here.

The stone column is old and crumbling now, once cared for as a navigation aid, but long since abandoned and neglected. I don't mind. In fact, I'm counting on no one visiting this place again for a long, long time.

A quick search of the ground below the column, and I find the right size stone. I reach into my back pocket and pull out a folded piece of paper. It's tattered, with edges torn, taped, and torn again. I unfold it and read through the twenty words written there decades ago. They read as true to me now as they did when I wrote them. I put the paper at the base of the column and set the stone on top of it to hold it there.

Then I turn away and walk back to my plane. I've covered 21,488 miles. Hawaii lies ahead, and California waits for my return.

Acknowledgments

I have enjoyed getting to know Bets and Miss E. while writing this book. My family deserves thanks for giving me the time I needed to watch their story grow and evolve. My wife gets special thanks for allowing the words "I'm working on my book" to trump all else.

Time to read is precious, so thanks must go to those who spent some of their reading time with this book when it was far from finished and to others whose comments and suggestions helped me know when it was: Andy, Donna, Sarah, Kathy, Hallie, and Tiffani.

Thanks also to Kathy M. for publishing guidance and advice, and to Maureen for her tireless editing.

About the Author

As an education specialist, father of two, and a former middle school English teacher, Brian Herberger is immersed in the world of young adult fiction. In his debut novel, Herberger builds on his knowledge of this genre, drawing on themes that have piqued the interest of his students for more than a decade as they too come of age. He draws on childhood memories of flying with his father and combines them with his love of history to create a story that is exciting, meaningful and fun.